AF473104

Order this book online at www.trafford.com/07-3078
or email orders@trafford.com

Most Trafford titles are also available at major online book retailers.

© Copyright 2008 Trevor Devas.
Co-authored by the late Rev. V. McKinley.
All rights reserved. No part of this publication may be reproduced, stored in a retrieval system, or transmitted, in any form or by any means, electronic, mechanical, photocopying, recording, or otherwise, without the written prior permission of the author.

Note for Librarians: A cataloguing record for this book is available from Library and Archives Canada at www.collectionscanada.ca/amicus/index-e.html

ISBN: 978-1-4251-6640-3

We at Trafford believe that it is the responsibility of us all, as both individuals and corporations, to make choices that are environmentally and socially sound. You, in turn, are supporting this responsible conduct each time you purchase a Trafford book, or make use of our publishing services. To find out how you are helping, please visit www.trafford.com/responsiblepublishing.html

Our mission is to efficiently provide the world's finest, most comprehensive book publishing service, enabling every author to experience success. To find out how to publish your book, your way, and have it available worldwide, visit us online at www.trafford.com/10510

www.trafford.com

North America & international
toll-free: 1 888 232 4444 (USA & Canada)
phone: 250 383 6864 • fax: 250 383 6804
email: info@trafford.com

The United Kingdom & Europe
phone: +44 (0)1865 722 113 • local rate: 0845 230 9601
facsimile: +44 (0)1865 722 868 • email: info.uk@trafford.com

10 9 8 7 6 5 4 3 2 1

INTRODUCTION

I am Trevor Devas, self employed in the Jewelry & Real Estate business in New York for the last twenty years.

I started Laugh & live Longer as a company because I felt that everyone of us should have a sense of humor in whatever one does for a living.

It helps us to change our attitude in life and move from a dead end job to a fulfilling career in life. It makes our life easier and we are able to handle our problems and challenges in life with a smile on our face and a prayer in our heart.

I learnt from the late Rev. Mckinley how he marketed and sold this book to his customers in his jewelry store and found that he made more friends and customers and sold more jewelry as a result of this approach in life.

Please visit my website at your convenience
www.laughlivelonger.com

I wish you enjoy reading my book, laugh & live longer and go through life with a smile on your face and a prayer in your heart.

TREVOR DEVAS
PRESIDENT
LAUGH & LIVE LONGER

Dedicated to late
Rev. Vern McKinley
who inspired me.

One man would do most anything to get his boy into Sunday School, except to go himself.

Don't let your parents down; they brought you up.

When two share a joy, it is doubled. When two share a sorrow, it is halved.

There are no victories without a conflict; no rainbows without a cloud.

Alcohol gives you a red nose, a white liver, a yellow streak, and a blue future.

Failure is the path of least resistance.

Brooding over trouble will make a perfect hatch.

Worry is like a rocking chair; it will give you something to do, but it won't carry you anywhere.

Defeat will not be bitter if you do not swallow it.

The best place to find a helping hand is on your wrist.

Those people who can, will do; those people who can't will criticize.

Some people never like anything, they dislike some things more than other things.

Drivers are safer when roads are dry; roads are safer when drivers are dry.

Many people who boast about their ancestors are like a potato vine: Their main good is under the ground.

It is good to be too busy to worry in the daytime, and too sleepy at night.

A Christian does two things: He gives and forgives.

A well-informed husband is one whose wife has just told him what she thinks of him.

By the time a family acquires a nest egg, inflation has turned it into chicken feed.

Juvenile delinquency is the result of parents trying to raise their kids without starting at the bottom.

Kids grow up to be rotten eggs when their parents are chicken.

Many a girl has found a knotty problem at the end of a smooth line.

Many a guy gets into deep water trying to make a splashing impression.

On the Sea of Matrimony, many a dream boat becomes a battleship.

Man has a hard time in life! No sooner does he bolt the door against the wolf than the stork flies in through the window.

The man who says his wife can't take a joke forgets himself.

A man without a lot of money may be a bad egg, but folks seldom take offense until he is broke.

A mother-in-law is an accessory after the pact.

Politics is the fine art of passing the buck after passing the hat.

A political job may not take much know-how, but it sure takes a lot of know who.

Make somebody happy today. Mind your own business.

Many people go to college so they can learn how to express their ignorance in scientific terms.

A man who criticizes the church should go sometime, to see if it has improved any.

Some have the gift of prophecy; others have the gift of gab.

Gold is tested by fire; man is tested by adversity.

Diamonds are chunks of carbon that stuck to their jobs.

The largest room is the room for improvement.

Your limitations are not what you want to do but can't; but what you ought to do and don't.

God will not look you over for medals, degrees or diplomas, but for scars.

We don't know the exact age of the human race, but we know it is old enough to know better.

When it comes to ideals in politics, people usually leave out the "i".

A new pair of shoes will not mend your wife's broken heart.

Some people think their weakness is inherited and their virtues are original.

Alcohol at its best reduces men to their worst.

If I convince you against your will, you are of the same opinion still.

Leisure is the time that people do things that are not useful.

If you have time to spare, don't spend it with people who don't.

The measure of a man's life is not the length of it, but how he spends it.

Our problem is not where life started, but where it will end.

In society it used to be who's who, now it is who's whose.

Many people are too religious to enjoy sin and too sinful to enjoy religion.

Where there is no conflict, there can be no triumph.

Move the letters, "D-I-E" from the word "DEPRESSION", and what you have left is "PRESS ON".

Forget yourself if you want to find happiness.

The greatest fault is when you believe you have none.

Any merchant who is willing to play ball with you plans to be the catcher.

If you have trouble supporting your family, you have more trouble if you don't.

Samson slew the Philistines with a jaw bone of an ass and a lot of men slew themselves with the same weapon.

One yard of performance is worth a mile of promise.

If you want some time to yourself, do the dishes.

Let the sermon of your life be illustrated by your conduct.

Flirting with sin can lead to romance.

One man is never contented with his lot until it is in the cemetery.

The farther you are from the wolf, the closer you are to the shepherd.

Don't hate sin too much to love men.

The man who speaks too quickly says something that he has never thought of.

It is what you learn after you know everything that counts.

The light of reason is often blown out.

If you think that you are going to wait until you can do something so well that nobody can find fault with it, it'll never be done.

While giving our children the thing that we didn't have, let us not forget to give them the things that we did have.

Death it not a period that ends the sentence of life. It is a comma to show there is more coming.

Don't go steady unless you are ready.

Live carefully, the soul you save could be your own.

You cannot strengthen the weak by weakening the strong.

You cannot help the poor by destroying the rich.

You cannot establish sound security on borrowed money.

It is not unconstitutional to pray silent.

We see what you hit, not what you aim at.

Be sincere whether you mean it or not.

Caution must be used in fishing, if you are the fish.

About the time you finish the school of experience, life is over.

Men stretch the truth like there was a shortage.

Dad don't mind his daughter going with that boy-Dad thinks they are both girls.

We must raise the salary of teachers so they won't envy the janitors.

If I act like a heel, I can't gain a toe hold on success.

Getting out of a rut is hard mountain climbing.

When you burn the candle at both ends, you are not bright.

When you are kicked from behind, you must be ahead.

Men marry poor girls and settle down. Girls marry rich men and settle up.

Love makes a woman make a man to make a fool of himself.

One tragedy is not getting what you want—Another is getting it.

You will easily reach your goal if you're going nowhere.

Panty hose makes a serious problem for Santa.

If your only scraps are what are brushed from the table, you have a happy home.

Some wear a strapless gown; others have a gownless strap.

Family trees should produce less nuts.

Why do you like people who agree with you and food that does not?

If we keep our resolutions secret, no one would know when you broke one.

You pay for cigarettes when you get them, and again when they get you.

You need experience to know how to use it.

Free speech is what we get in a polital campaign.

After all is said and done, it hath been the woman that said it and the man that done it.

We enjoy our children's pets until the pets have children.

The best board of education is dad's paddle.

At one time when a kid was called into the principal's office, he was in trouble–Today the principal is in trouble.

You are known by the company you think no one knows about.

Rumors seem to get around even when they have no leg to stand on.

If the only thing you have on the string is a kite, you are at the right age.

Money won't buy happiness–Some add credit cards.

You never know what you can do until you have to undo it.

When we give 'til it hurts, we are too sensitive to pain.

Your train of thought may be a train of empties.

Science can't prove why a child can't walk around a mud hole.

Heredity proves that all the faults come from the other parent.

Men have two choices; all the money or alimony.

When you pay repossessed love out on installment, that is called alimony.

You are ahead if you are kicked from the rear.

If you want to start at the top, dig a well.

I don't ever remember a day that I failed to survive.

We may have to pay for the car and finance the insurance.

A man is seldom criticized for not talking.

Those who earn their living should form the nation's budget.

There's one thing worse than growing old; that is not to have the chance.

If you want to know how to spend money, ask him who has none.

If success turns your head, it should wring your neck.

Some make money-Others earn it.

If you offer me the world on a silver platter, I'll just take the platter.

It is easier to criticize than to understand.

Employers want to know what kids do after graduation.

A teenager quits asking where he came from and quits telling where he is going.

We have the right to say it, but we don't always have the courage.

We need a peace pipe with a pilot light.

We have a lot of wide open spaces - surrounded by teeth.

The girl who comes out second in a beauty contest is called a raving beauty.

Teenagers in love don't want advice.

A working committee has three men-Two are absent.

Americans started with nothing and now we have $200,000,000, 000.00 less than nothing.

If you want safe cars, pad the bumpers.

Silence is seldom found in women, men, boys, or girls.

To a man catching the train, "If you turn left, you will be right. If you turn right, you will be left."

If you want to share the flowers, help plant the seed.

Puppy love is putting on the dog.

We need fewer needs.

The first step of a ladder is stronger-It has the most of us on it.

Optimists should be salesmen-Pessimists must run the credit branch.

In public speaking the biggest mistake some preachers make is to open their mouths.

If courtesy is contagious, we need an epidemic.

We can argue about things without understanding them.

Mouthwash helps our breath-Kindness the disposition.

Some thought and never did-Some did and never thought-Others thought they did.

Write down what you did yesterday! It will make you do more tomorrow.

Some people are bothered by temptations that they can't find.

If you want to teach the kid to count, don't give the same allowance.

Bright people's parents believe in heredity.

It gives me a headache for you to wear your halo.

The more patience I have, the more others use me.

Preachers get carried away by the quality of their voice-But not far enough.

It is okay to prepare a sermon if you would prepare a stopping place.

Hunting for an easy way to make a living can become tiresome.

People don't believe it is better to give than to receive unless they can get a tax deduction.

Man labored with the sweat of the brow until we got air conditioning and welfare.

A college teacher has his ignorance organized.

Where is the college that offers a degree in the art of loafing?

Don't make a problem out of solving a problem.

Many detours on the road to success.

You can't get ahead if you don't have one.

Many busy people are just dying to get into the cemetery.

Self control can carry a credit card and not use it.

Silence is a good way for you to hide ignorance.

Surprise your husband - Compliment him.

Discard your halo-Take the weight off your mind.

Go into poverty-That's where the money is.

Straighten out a child by bending him over.

Through our mistakes, we learn to blame them on others.

We were younger in the old days.

Men are basically honest, until an opportunity appears.

The way of a transgressor is not lonesome.

Pollution helps politics.

Take your vacation before another postage hike.

Some kids learn how to throw a tantrum.

When a match gets lit, it loses its head-Same with a man.

Many men retire before they begin to work.

Money won't buy happiness, but it helps you hunt.

Before you retire, watch television in the daytime two weeks.

Don't seek the benefit of the doubt. There is none.

Some people have too much of the world to enjoy religion and too much religion to enjoy the world.

God did not deliver Daniel from the lion's den; Daniel was delivered in the lions den.

Some people get married on puppy love. That is why they lead a dog's life.

So many people are so busy laying up for a rainy day, they forget to enjoy the sunshine.

It is better to be silent like a fool than to talk like one.

They used to sing, "Sweet Hour of Prayer" in church, now the favorite seems to be, "Just a little talk with Jesus Makes it Right".

Don't say all you know, but know all you say.

It takes 68 gallons of water to Baptize people; it takes two drops to keep them out of church.

Some use religion just like a bus; they ride on it when it goes their way.

Too many churches have loose living and tight giving.

The government taxes our clothes off our back and then bans nudism.

Live through the day in such a way that you will not be afraid to talk in your sleep at night.

A good name is won by many acts and is lost by one.

We saw a sign on an old car: "Out of date but out of debt".

While some are singing, "Plunge out into the deep", others are singing, "You're drifting too far from the shore".

Jesus wore a crown of thorns that I may wear a crown of life.

On Sunday morning, some folk sing, "O, WHY NOT TONIGHT"

You are not held accountable for your weaknesses, but you are held accountable for messing with them.

I am not ruined by living in the world, but by the world living in me.

We generate fear when we are idle.

Before you can become good, you must first discover that you have been bad.

Telephone number to the Garden of Eden: ADAM 8-1-2.

Happiness is one thing that multiplies by division.

A modern husband is a do-it-yourself man with a get-it-done wife.

Inflation is a state of affairs when you never had it so good-or parted with it so fast.

Many a husband looks run-down because of the bills his wife runs up.

Some Christians are like lightening bugs-just a flicker now and then.

An Englishman, on arrival in this country, remarked how well the parents obeyed their children.

Many people dream about tomorrow, complain about today, not considering that today is yesterday's tomorrow.

A man's Sunday self and week day self are like two halves of a round trip ticket-not good if detached.

Quite often when a man thinks his mind is getting broader it is only his conscience stretching.

In the "good ole days", we only feared attack from the Indians.

People who get something for nothing always want more.

A man's life is twenty years of having his mother ask him where he is going, forty hears of having his wife ask the same question and, at the end, having the mourners wondering too.

The greatness of many a man is merely the possession of a clever wife.

The hardest thing to explain to the wife about money matters is that money matters.

Financial success is a wonderful thing. You meet such interesting relatives.

A mother-in-law many times is a puzzle with crosswords.

Some people have mouths like a hamburger stand-open day and night.

If you think life begins at 40, you will miss a lot.

I don't minimize my faults by magnifying yours.

There are more overstuffed things in the American homes, other than the furniture.

No one has enough money to buy his past.

If you want to live in the house of many mansions, make your reservations now.

Character is tested by wealth and poverty.

Politics help to simplify history. Anything bad that happens during an administration, they inherited. Anything good, they invented.

The hand-shaking done by Presidential candidates provides enough energy to milk all the tax payers for the next four years.

A woman may believe that faith will move mountains, but she finds it hard to believe it moves surplus fat.

A little bit of faith and a strong log can cause me to cross a creek but a lot of faith and a rotten log will cause me to fall into the creek.

If I do what I should, I will not have time to do what I should not.

A married man should never get so busy earning his salt that he forgets his sugar.

Why complain that your days are only a few and then act like there is no end to them?

In my Bible, I find the words, "Trust", and "Peace" a hundred times, but I have never found the word, "Worry".

God allows storms to happen only to prove that He is the only real shelter.

Any preacher who serves God for money will serve the devil for a little more money.

Don't be so stingy that you would use second-hand material to build air castles.

We don't want borrowed trouble to be returned.

The world's disappointed man is the man that gets what's coming to him.

Worry is to pull tomorrow's clouds over today's sunshine.

Why don't you live so men will want your autograph instead of your fingerprints?

God is big enough to be concerned with your smallest need.

The modern conscience is made with a lever to throw it out of gear.

Having his name on the church roll doesn't make a man a Christian, any more than owning a piano makes him a musician.

Sometimes nothing may be the best thing to say.

An education is teaching a child how to talk and then how to keep quiet.

Prayer should have never been taken out of school, because it caused some of us to graduate.

Everything gets easier by practice except getting up in the morning.

Doers and deciders are often criticized, but oddly enough by people who are usually neither doers or deciders.

What is the human race? It is woman chasing man.

God said: I AM only a prayer away.

No one is too big to be courteous, but some are too little.

Man says, "Show me and I will believe", but God says, "Believe and I will show you".

A friend comes in when all the world goes out.

Don't consider what your friend does but what he intended to do.

You don't clean off dirt with mud, neither do you heal an evil word with another evil word. Some people after they break a habit mount the pieces and frame them.

Worry hovers around where faith has fainted.

God did not give ten suggestions. He gave ten commandments.

I am not interested in where you have been, but I am interested in where you are going.

The greatest compliment God can give me is to prune me.

A word once spoken can never be recalled.

When you criticize your church you criticize yourself; you are part of it.

Some drop a penny into the offering and then expect a hundred dollar sermon.

Some men grow when elected to office others swell up.

If you hide your religion you may lose it.

He has most trouble who looks for it.

You don't need mountain faith to move a mustard seed.

If you are going to tell your wife everything, do it before the other person does.

You are not broke if you still have five senses.

The hard boiled men are still just half baked.

A bridge only hits a car in self defense.

When a man falls in love, a lady usually helps him out.

A rich fool is a wanted man.

Some keep an ox close to a ditch so they can push him in.

You must climb the steps of success one at a time; there are no elevators.

Would you prepare for your first Sunday in Heaven by missing Sunday School, your last Sunday on earth?

Your absence from Sunday School is usually a vote to close it.

Work eight hours; sleep eight hours; but not the same eight hours.

The man who has never raised kids can tell others how.

The Lord puts the Church in the world; the devil tries to put the world in the Church.

A "dream house" costs more than you dreamed it would.

Old women don't care where the husband goes just so she doesn't have to go.

A loafer says he can't live on the wages he refuses. He keeps living.

Drinking milk does not make you a calf. Going to church doesn't necessarily make you a Christian either.

If you are smarter than you look, you should be.

Uncle Sam takes all you have and gives others all they have.

Barbed wire fences protect the property without obstructing the view–same with some modern dresses.

Inflation makes everything valuable but money.

Friends are those who borrow books and set wet glasses on them.

Do you believe in the hereafter? The here determines the after.

If I buy what I don't need, I'll need what I can't buy.

There is no right time to do a wrong thing.

The bouquet I hand to myself looks like weeds to others.

The road to ruin is paved.

To think of dying an old maid is not so bad, but living that way.

Self-made men worship their maker.

A bed is like a habit, easy to get into but hard to get out of.

People only go to an attorney when trouble comes-some treat the Lord the same way.

He that mindeth his own business will soon have a business to mind of his own.

Operations once left scars-now the hospital bills do.

This nation has turned out some great preachers-Others not so great should be turned out.

There is one reliable truth-The knowledge some men are unreliable.

Girl: "Lord, if you can't improve me, don't worry, I'm enjoying myself."

Sign on the moon: "Your tax dollars at work."

What went with the old-fashioned men that took care of the public's money?

Some grieve for what they have lost-Some for what they never had.

Don't be conceited and you will get credit for knowing more than you do.

Some men have a heart of gold-So does a hard boiled egg.

A politician or weatherman can tell you today what will happen tomorrow. The next day he can explain why it never took place.

Education helps men to get into intelligent problems.

Medicine holds men's interest while nature heals them.

We judge a man by the company most people don't know he is keeping.

Ask about the cost of a new one and your old car will run better.

The drive should forget the girl and hug the road.

It may take all kinds of people to make the world, but there are too many of some kinds.

It is hard to play tennis without raising a racket.

If you can't make donations, nor qualify for charity, you are in the middle class.

If you can't say nice things about your friends, get new ones.

Be more careful in selecting your materials if you are a self-made man.

If you do what you are forced to do with a smile, you are cooperating.

Why not put off until tomorrow what you already put off 'til today?

Happiness comes by work.

Life is what you make it, by the help of your wife and Uncle Sam.

The man who entertains salesmen and visitors while we work is an executive.

A good idea is valuable if it is put in action.

The man who watches the way people are going and steps in front of them is a leader.

It is better to not know anything and know it than to not know anything and not know it.

Knowledge without wisdom is dangerous.

Why know how to live everyone's life by your own?

The boss would not be a crank if we had more self-starters.

Let's tell the FBI that the senators have been passing some bad bills.

We could brush with the old toothpaste and have less commercials.

Sometimes snap judgement comes unfastened.

If we call driving work, many drivers will slow down.

Grandma had to push grandpa to wash dishes. Granddaughter pushes a button.

Everything in the home these days are controlled by switches except the children.

You make the most of life when most of it is gone.

When a man wipes his windshield at a drive-in move, the honeymoon is over.

When a man proposes on his knees, it is hard to get back on his feet.

Men call their mistakes experience.

Live so men will not cheer when you die.

Some men spend all their life becoming famous, then wear sunglasses so no one will recognize them.

If the statements of both candidates are true, neither is fit for office.

He who laughs last has a thick skull.

Don't be so democratic you won't know right and wrong.

A self-conceited saint is worse than a self-confessed sinner.

You are not what you should be 'til you do what you should do.

Truth will convince a man or make him mad.

We need a mirror that helps you see yourself as others see you.

Some stop at nothing when it comes to an offering.

If you want to feel better off, ride a horse bareback.

Sound your horn when in danger, or Gabriel will do it for you.

If money grew on trees, lazy men wouldn't shake the limb.

Why is it we never have time to do things right, but always time to do them over?

Talk is cheap if it is not long distance.

Why leave the dock minutes before your ship comes in?

An alcoholic need not worry about his future. He hasn't much.

Free advice could cost most if taken.

It is harder to work your way out of a jam than to talk yourself into it.

Your wife tells you what to do. Your secretary does it.

A live wire needs good connections.

You help the other man if you will fix it so he won't need to help you.

If you use religion as a cloak, you will be warm enough without one in the next world.

Most men never have growing pains in the head.

Even a tea kettle can sing when it is in hot water.

I'd rather be beat in the right than succeed in wrong.

You can't make your husband tender hearted by keeping him in hot water.

If you want to be a marksman, shoot and then draw the circles.

Conceal how little you think of others and how much you think of self.

The size of what makes you mad shows your size.

If it is not worth saying, let a hippie set it to music.

Enthusiasm for work is good if you are the boss.

In all your affairs, make your wife a silent partner.

The man who is too tired to help at home plays golf or watches T.V.

You have no time for the answers if you keep up with the problems.

Don't let work take too much of your time.

If you want a lift, get your wife to tell about the boy she turned down to get to you.

The best time to buy something was last year.

Will power helps you to eat only one peanut.

Only drunk men think liquor will bring prosperity.

The Lord giveth; IRS taketh away.

When we live in an all-electric home, everything is charged.

A preacher said, "Will all those who are present stand, please".

A real friend does not believe what he hears about you.

The more you hang around temptation, the better it looks.

A man becomes crooked by dodging the issue.

Inflation may cause us to carry our groceries in our pockets and our money in push carts.

The less a woman deserves alimony, the more it is worth to not have her around.

Life is a one way street to one of two places.

Soft soap removes a dirty look.

Old senators never die. They just spend away.

When I make a fool of myself, my friends don't think it is permanent.

We can't see electricity but we see the light. It is the same with faith.

If you don't want to lose your religion, take it to work with you.

If you want to gamble on your life, take out insurance-Insurance is betting you will die before the company believes you will.

Doctors cover their mistakes with sod–Brides with mayonnaise.

Stay on your job and pay taxes. Thousands in Washington are depending on you.

It is not good scandal unless it is bad.

Women wear rings to show they are married- Men wear run-over shoes.

Some count what condemns them in the Bible as a misprint.

It is hard to hide what you don't have.

You don't build a reputation on good intentions.

What counts is business you hold rather than the business you get.

I'll never get anywhere if I believe I am already there.

Two ants at a golf course said, "If we don't get on the ball, we'll get killed."

A teenager said, "How can such stupid parents produce such a cupid girl?"

If you think it is best to leave well enough alone, why build a statue to a dead man?

Efficiency experts would cut the Ten Commandments down to five.

It seems most everything in the home these days are controlled by switches except the kids.

You get out of it what you put in your pocketbook or mirror.

If a meek man inherits the earth, will he stay meek?

If you want to make good, do it where you are.

Some pedestrians don't look where they go after they are in an ambulance.

Prosperity also has a reverse gear.

If man descended from an ape, when will he quit descending?

It is hard in the business life to attend to your own.

One lady in church testified she was proud she was humble.

Opportunity knocks and Prosperity rings the bell.

If politicians keep calling each other liars, people will begin to believe them.

Suppose there are so many satellites in space, the flying saucers can't get through!

A man's circulation is stopped when he is in jail.

The bird that can't fly is a jail bird.

A bachelor looks before he leaps. That is why he does not leap.

What you learn after you "know it all" is education.

Many drivers are in such a hurry to get to the next state, they go into the next world.

If you want to be happy, count your blessings and not your cash.

Why should I condemn myself when others will do it for me?

To buy hay for a dead cow is similar to alimony.

Some know how to live everyone's life but their own.

The hen that lays the smallest egg does the most cackling.

The horn of plenty starts some men on a toot.

It isn't what you get for your work, but what you become by it that counts.

Look for a wife who already has a fur coat and her tonsils out.

When I am robbed by worry, it is an inside job.

Is stealing a kiss petty larceny or grand?

When you are afraid, you are a coward. When I am afraid I am cautious.

When your ship comes in, your relatives will be sure to be on board.

Our money goes further today than ever before. It has gone to the moon.

Why stick to your gun if it is not loaded?

The reason you can't take it with you, it's all gone.

Bull throwers in Spain are "Senors". Here they are "Senators".

Do you get a poor reception listening to your conscience?

A fatal accident is when you run into debt.

The woman that talks by the yard and thinks by the inch must be removed by the foot.

If your car starts with a jerk, why don't you just change drivers?

Jumping at conclusions is the only mental exercise some people have.

It is looking downward that makes one dizzy.

Even if you are on the right track you will get run over if you just sit there.

A small deed well done is far grander than the most sincere wish never carried out.

Even the woodpecker owes his success to the fact that he uses his head.

Nothing ruins the truth like stretching it.

Just a short prayer will reach the throne if you don't live too far away.

Man is made to pray and not to bray.

Some preachers are called, some sent, and some just packed up and went.

A diplomat is a man who remembers a woman's birthday but forgets her age.

He who throws mud loses ground.

The following shows you when you should become alarmed: If you find yourself beginning to love any pleasure better than your prayers; any book better than the Bible; any place better than the House of God; any table better than the Lord's table; any person better than Christ; or any indulgence better than hope of heaven.

Some are hiding their light under a bushel, when a thimble would serve just as well.

Be friendly with the folks you know, if it wasn't for them, you would be a total stranger.

If you deceive me once, shame on you. If you deceive me twice, Shame on me.

People are now in hell who wasted time trying to find where Cain got his wife.

Some of the biggest lies ever told are at funerals and on tomb-stones.

Temptation is Satan knocking on the door; sin is opening the door and letting him in.

One lady said that she would come to church if she ever got straightened out. One day she got straightened out and they rolled her in, in a casket.

You may give until you are rich, and keep until you are poor.

The preacher said so many good things about her dead husband at the funeral that the widow sent one of her children up to be sure that it was him.

There is no food value in wild oats.

Man may not have come from a monkey, but many of them are going to the dogs.

We must spend money to make character, but we must not spend character to make money.

Some people will never come to church until they ride in a hearse.

It is better to say a good thing about a bad fellow, than to say a bad thing about a good fellow.

Rivers and men become crooked by following the line of least resistance.

Many a fellow who starts out with a bottle ends up in the can.

Alimony is taxation without representation.

Some fellows claim they shouldn't be forced to pay alimony, because they committed matrimony while in a state of temporary insanity.

Some women treat their husband like fifteen cents and then demand thousands when another woman gets him.

The best way a husband can make his wife suspicious with an anniversary gift is to give her just what she wants.

Half-truths are like half a brick-they can be thrown further.

A wooden anniversary is the day on which a man realizes what a blockhead he was.

Silver anniversary for some people is the day on which the couple celebrates the fact that the first 25 years of their married life is finally over.

I write down everything I want to remember. That way, instead of spending a lot of time trying to remember what it is I wrote down, I spend the time looking for the paper I wrote it on.

Some claim the most impressive evidence of their tolerance is a golden wedding anniversary.

Some girls can only be as pretty as a picture if they are well-painted.

Computer print-out: "I am your friendly computer. Your account is past due. If payments aren't made, I will have to refer this to a human."

A girl who is beautiful to look at, may be hard to look after.

When the roof of the computer room begins to leak, it causes water on the brain.

A man will go a long way to save a face, but a girl just goes to the drug store.

In a motel office: "We confirm your reservation in 50 seconds or we whip the computer".

When girls start fishing for me, they try all sorts of artificial lures.

Just pretending to be rich keeps some people poor.

A pretty girl may be like a melody, but after you marry her, you have to face the music.

The easier a girl is to look at, the harder most men look.

Everybody makes mistakes, but some give them assistance.

The best way for a man to remember his wife's birthday is to forget it just once.

Most of us accumulate birthdays faster than we learn to act our age.

Women don't observe birthdays-they merely preserve them.

My mechanic said, "Let me put it this way-if you car was a horse, it would have to be shot".

It's amazing that when a brother and sister has a birthday, if they are twins, he boasts of fifty while she admits only to thirty.

Many a bride, although given away, turns out to be a most expensive gift.

Just by putting a ring on her finger, many a man winds up under her thumb.

Many a girl has married a mink only to discover later that what she really got was a skunk.

It takes a lot of cooking to make a marriage pan out.

When the devil catches you idle, he will try to put you to work.

Anything we gain by yielding to sin is not worth what we have to give up.

God has no bigger job for the man who is not faithfully doing what he can.

Money is funny. You have to be dead to get your face on it, but very much alive to get your hands on it.

The political bee buzzes loudest around the candidates for office, but it is usually the public that gets stung.

We took the country away from the Indians, who scalped us and gave it to the politicians, who skin us.

Fat folks know that the reducing business is still being done on a large scale.

It is ironic that when a girl starves herself until she gets her desired weight back, every fellow she knows wants to take her out to dinner.

The reason for the expression, "cool million", is that after taxes, the balance ain't so hot.

Do you realize that 60 million calories are consumed during every station break on television?

When a husband comes home late, many wives want to know where he has been before she tells him where to go.

The way to a woman's heart is through the jeweler's window.

You can trust some people to the ends of the earth and others not until they get there.

A credit card is a convenient way to spend money you wish you had.

Never argue with your dentist-It may result in bad fillings.

Some can't understand our public figures because of public figures.

A lot comes out at a bridge table that is not in the cards.

The least thing you can do for your wife is to buy her a bikini.

If a couple live happily ever after, they were not after much.

This is your country-Love it or leave it.

A girl is sometimes dynamite if you drop her.

An elevator operator has a lot of ups and downs.

Add another star to our flag to represent the confused state.

It is not what the world is coming to, but when.

Taxes are staggering, but never go down.

A happy ending at the movie is when the couple behind you stop smooching.

Times are hard for those who seek soft jobs.

Old golfers never die, they just get tee'd off.

A banker lends you an umbrella while the sun shines and takes it back when it rains.

Nobody stays young, but some act childish forever.

If you wait long enough, good times will come to the other fellow.

A fool and his money are soon parted-Others wait until time to pay taxes.

To err is human-Some find a better excuse.

The world is better because some men lived and because some died.

What gives you away is what you give into.

Language is the dress worn by your thoughts.

The drugs when I was a teenager were sulphur and grease.

Today's taxes are yesterday's political promises.

To support a U.S. soldier, it takes the wool of one sheep, the meat of a cow, and the hide of two tax payers.

A hamburger costs more if it has another name.

Nearly all physicians specialize-some specialize on banking.

Maybe Texas should withdraw from the union and apply for foreign aid.

The easiest way to find a policeman is "unexpectedly".

People save pennies because there is nothing they can buy with them.

We get out of life what we put in it-less taxes.

Money talks and it says goodbye.

Intuition makes a woman contradict her husband before he says a word.

Kids are not guilty of thoughtless mischief when they plan the mischief.

Some college kids try to clean up the world's troubles when they can't clean up their own room.

Some men have ulcers and yet are not successful.

Young people start life looking for a pot of gold at the end of the rainbow-Old people have a pot.

Young marrieds believe in "planned parenthood". They live with their parents.

If you want to get rid of an enemy make a friend of him.

If you wake up and find you are successful you probably have not been asleep.

If anything will go without saying, let it go.

Don't pray for rain and then grumble about the mud.

Between what you can't do and what you won't do you do nothing.

Many women listen to what their husbands say when he talks in his sleep.

Were we supposed to talk more than listen we would have one ear and two tongues.

Money the rich has called capital; getting it from him is labor.

Many people live in fear-of bending an IBM card.

Test your strength-life a mortgage.

Be different - act natural.

Many people enter the door, but continue knocking.

Don't judge one's horsepower by his exhaust.

The family that smokes together chokes together.

You will see people in Heaven you don't expect to see-others will be surprised to see you too.

The Marshal plan takes money from the poor of a rich country and gives it to the rich of a poor country.

If you can walk to the welfare office, you can walk to work.

The Supreme Court may declare all of us unconstitutional.

Spending money is as easy as it looks.

Free advice is worth about what it costs.

I fell several times before I learned to walk.

A little bush may become a big oak that started with one little acorn.

If you lose your head you probably won't miss it.

Even a postage stamp sticks to one thing until it reaches its goal.

You should make some deposits before you try to cash checks on the bank of heaven.

You cannot tell by the way the horn sounds how much gasoline is in a car.

Why would the elder brother weep more over the fatted calf than over the stray son?

If you stay on a wild goose chase all your life you will never feather your nest.

No one likes to be stopped in the middle of a sentence, but a convict.

When you are in the valley, read the Sermon on the Mount.

You don't stop playing because you are old; you are old because you stopped playing.

You will not be proud of your child that follows your example if you stay away from church.

Your religion will not cure people if it makes you look sick.

A short life in the saddle is better than a long life by the fire.

Satan will try to get us to study the past and future, so much that we will not have contentment for the present.

If you look for faults look in a looking glass instead of a telescope.

The tomorrow you worried about yesterday is here.

If you think you know everything you are at your journey's end.

Many never leave their first love when they are self-centered.

Everyone who slings mud has dirty hands.

If you don't want to be shot at don't be a target.

If someone gives you the big head, the next fellow will stick a pin in it.

A bootlegger is ashamed of his customers.

Do you have a good opinion of yourself? You may be a poor judge of human nature.

Laziness travels so slowly that she is overtaken by poverty.

Some people are afraid to sell their parrot.

Many people who lose their temper quickly find it.

It is a bad sign if your child loves a baby sitter more than you.

I heard that a man warned the people in the show that a fellow at the front was going to kill the fellow in there with his wife; about fifty men slipped out the back.

Noisy water is usually not deep enough to drown anyone.

It takes hot water to bring out the good in tea.

The reason that keeps you from church is the same reason the church is necessary.

Imaginary trouble is made real by telling them.

I don't know exactly the human race's age, but it is old enough to know better.

A "brat" is a child who acts like your own but belongs to a neighbor.

"Soft soap" in the pulpit will not cleanse the sinner in the pew.

Many a hungry soul abides in a well-fed body.

Beauty without virtue is a rose without fragrance.

An exaggeration is a truth that has lost its temper.

He who practices what he preaches may have to put in some over time.

Marriage is either a holy wedlock or an unholy deadlock.

You are young only once, but you can stay immature indefinitely.

God in His wisdom has made the mouth to close, and the ear to remain open.

"The bee is seldom complimented for making honey-it's just criticized for stinging!"

A smile is the lighting system of the face and the heating system of the heart.

It is sad that the only respect some people have for Sunday is to wear their best clothes.

Cosmetics: Preparations used by teenagers to make them look older sooner and by their mothers to make them look younger longer.

There is no right way to do a wrong thing.

To grieve over sin is one thing; to repent is altogether another!

Of all things you wear, your expression is the most important.

If you have a half hour to spare, don't spend it with someone who hasn't.

Valuable advice comes when you have to ask for it.

For twenty years I could not do anything big for God, so I decided to do 10,000 little things.

The Lord made a handout of my fist.

A boy said, "We killed a bear. Pa shot him."

A fly on an elephant's ear said, "Didn't we shake that bridge as we come over it."

A woman said to her husband, "Why can't we pull together as the mules pulling this wagon?" The man said, "there is only one tongue between them."

Our heaviest burden is something that never happens.

It takes dirt to grow things-That is why gossip thrives.

When you shoot at a target, you must allow for the wind-It is the same in hearing a political speech.

Say "Nice doggy" 'til you find a rock.

The hang-ups of a boy does not include clothes.

Some say, "Can I afford to marry?" Others say, "Can I get by without a wife that works?"

It is too late to ruin the past.

Give some women enough rope and they will skip.

Inflation has affected feathers - "Down is up."

It takes a long time to become an overnight success.

A new wife can open cans or use a credit card.

Two women say little-The quiet ones and gabby ones.

Some law makers passed the bar-Some are still there.

The straight and narrow path gets a lot of wear along the edges.

Fault finders would be miserable in Heaven.

God sends us the storms to prove that He is the only real shelter.

They tell us little babies are angels, but their wings grow shorter as their legs grow longer.

On a tombstone: "He kept his tears to himself and shared his joy with others."

I will accept advise if it does not intercept my plans.

True sympathy comes from suffering.

A man should spend money if it causes him to build his character, but it is wrong to spend character to make money.

You have the wrong slant if you are looking down your nose at other people.

Little white lies pick up a lot of dirt as they travel.

I believe we should walk hand-in-hand even if we don't see eye-to-eye.

Please God even if it does offend the devil.

Jesus was in better company in the stable than He would be today in some Christmas parties.

Jesus would have had a lonely time here on earth had He refused to associate with sinners.

The Lord will give you work if you keep your tools sharp.

The devil may go to and fro but the Lord is already there.

The world is a gigantic jigsaw puzzle with a piece missing. YOU.

Theology is the truth on ice, but evangelism is the truth on fire.

If you seem to have difficulty meeting people why don't you try picking up their check?

Saying very little comes from thinking twice.

Some members get all they can and can all they get and then sit on the can.

Why advertise the banquet when you have no food?

I am only a prayer away.

A hair in the head is worth two in the brush.

If you cannot get an offering out of the people, why don't you threaten them. Tell them that you are going to sing.

Man says, "Show me and I will believe," but God says, "Believe and I will show you."

A tree never stops growing until it dies. Some women are not much different.

You don't clean off dirt with mud and neither do you heal an evil word with another evil word. Some people after they break a habit mount the pieces and frame them.

My friend knows that I am not perfect but he treats me like I am.

Horse sense is not hitched to a wagging tongue.

Some men will never put their best foot forward until they get the other foot in hot water.

Some men will never repent of their sins until they are caught.

A married man should never get so busy earning his salt that he forgets his sugar.

Why complain that your days are only a few and then act like there is no end to them?

It is possible for a man to differ with me and still be wrong.

The secret of health is to eat onions, and keep it secret.

What used to bring shame now brings television programs.

Some enjoy religion. Some endure it.

We need yard grass that will grow only an inch tall.

A man takes a day off on his birthday. A woman takes a year off.

When you feel your corns more than your oats, you are growing old.

In baseball the bases get loaded, in football, the fans do.

It's not dying an old maid that's bad. It's living that way.

I want to drive so my license will expire before I do.

Has tax forms made more liars than golf?

Are you more sure of what you don't like than what you like?

If you know nothing, why repeat it?

Give some drivers seat belts- Others strait jackets.

Is your expenditure of speech bigger than your income of ideas?

Things aren't so bad if you once get used to being nervous.

Don't trouble your friends with your troubles–Tell them to your enemies.

If you say, "I'll do it tomorrow", you probably said that yesterday.

Some women can shop all day without much sense.

A man stops trying to improve his neighbors when he sees himself.

How can you mind your business if you have no mind or business?

Some men would do right if they thought it was wrong.

Your good looks may be ruined when you sneer-at a larger man.

The women who put on the best clothes put off the most creditors.

A sunny life is not made by a shady business.

Drive like you owned the car–not the road.

If you want to keep your boys on the farm, do the work.

A canoe does better if paddled from the back. It is the same with a kid.

A woman in love thinks one man is different to the others.

You can float a rumor easier than you can sink it.

When a businessman started to repossess a washing machine, the woman said, "That salesman told us it would pay for itself in six months".

One preacher didn't like chicken and he backslid.

A good frame of mind will help you be in the picture of health.

Women can do what men can–except listen.

The women who follow the styles may go barefooted up to their necks.

Why worry? You may have as much future as you can stand.

People want to be in front of the bus, back of the church, the middle of the road, on top of the world, but not under the weather.

There are legal ways to be dishonest. Why be a criminal?

How can a married man get a bachelor's degree?

Some adults tell teenagers to "get lost", others tell them, "find yourself".

Why tie your dog and let your boy run loose?

You can hurt some men by lying on them-you can hurt others by telling the truth.

Many give advice which they don't use.

A clock went wrong and struck twenty- a man yelled, "It's later than it's ever been".

Our highways are so crowded we can't use them.

It is easy to find the silver lining in the other man's cloud.

We measure a man by the size of the thing that can get him angry.

If you want to keep a boy out of hot water, put soap in it.

We only see our shadow when the sun shines-that's when we see some kind of friends.

God wants us to play the game and He will keep the score.

Do not always follow a good example-look at the counterfeiter.

If the nations would stack their arms, we could stack our dollars.

Later comes too soon when I buy now.

Sympathize with a dog and he will follow you-a man is the same way.

Telephones used to be a convenience.

It is good to hear both sides of an argument - it is better to hear the end of one.

We do our best saving money when we have none.

Illness causes unhappy married lives. Some couples are sick of one another.

If you want a clean mind, change it each day.

The husband can get the last word if it is his last will.

They say a farmer sent the IRS a quarter .25 cent piece and said he would pay by the quarter.

Loose tongues stretch the truth.

If you can make yourself popular while you give the people gifts out of their own money, you are a politician.

Swelled heads shrink influence.

A man who talks in your sleep is a preacher.

Some dresses are too short or she is not in them far enough.

A labor-saving device is tomorrow.

Hold up your chin but don't turn up your nose.

We see unexpected things on the freeway-the exit we should have taken.

If we keep going deeper in the hole, the reds won't have to bury us.

Soon we can keep the tax and let the IRS have the income.

Television makes it so you have to wake up so you can go to bed.

Good luck comes to men who don't depend on it to survive.

Some men want a well-informed wife - others want a well-formed wife.

The best time for a cold shower is some other time.

Bachelors don't know what married bliss is-many married men don't either.

Eat, drink and be merry, for you may not have any credit to-morrow.

Flattery is a fool's food.

Some people buy a load of dirt for their yard, some for their library.

Some young people are spoiled, Some old people naturally smell that way.

Perfect mates come in gloves.

What you don't know does not help you.

What the hippie eats turns to hair.

We get the pitch too high when we sing our own praise.

Air pollution can't be controlled in election years only.

Always stop talking just before people want you to.

God created the world in six days-Uncle Sam couldn't have done it in 6,000 years.

If you can find a machine that will do half your work, buy two.

The mortality rate is 100 per cent on drinkers and non -drinkers.

Don't expect a million dollar answer to a .25 cent prayer.

Power of love should replace the love of power.

Sometimes you must do unto others a long time before they do it to you.

Flattery will get us no where when we spend it on ourselves.

Some spread cheer - others just spread.

Your neighbor's troubles are not as bad as yours, but their kids are worse than yours.

A revolving charge account makes me dizzy.

The one who is off key has the loudest voice-in the choir and in politics.

Balance your budget - rotate the creditors.

If we have nothing as our target, we hit it.

What really counts is what visitors say as they drive off.

We know a wise man by what he does not say.

We tax those who behave to take care of the one's who don't.

Discipline is what we put on one end of the child to teach the other.

In Summer our pool is filled with our neighbor's kids- in the fall, it is filled with their leaves.

You can smile when all goes wrong if you can blame it on someone.

If at first you don't succeed, you will get a lot of free advice.

Teenage marriage begins an adult education.

If you give until it hurts, you will be sensitive to pain.

The Bell Telephone tolls for you-if you are in the bath tub.

It takes all kinds of people to make a world-why don't they begin?

The biggest liars are those who lie to themselves.

Many who have presence of mind have absence of thought.

How can you tell where you are going if you don't know where you are?

Some churches practice liberalism except during offerings.

Don't talk with a full mouth or an empty head.

A good husband stands by his wife in troubles caused by marriage.

If she always agrees with you, she will lie to others too.

One fisherman does not lie when he calls another one a liar.

Some women are the size they can wear anything, but they won't.

Some are willing only to serve on the advisory board.

Be content with what you have, not with what you are.

I admire the wisdom of he who asks advice of me.

Ignorance is more expensive than education.

A woman will listen all day if you talk to her about herself.

Tears don't always mean compassion. A block of ice weeps.

I don't just take what comes. I go after what I want.

The narrow road has no traffic jams.

Mother had rather her daughter look like her than act like her.

Some may bottle their way to the bottom. Some battle their way to the top.

The "I" strain that is incurable is called conceit.

The only worry I have is under my hat.

If a skeptic thought seeing was believing, he'd close his eyes.

She said she was as good as half the people in church-which half?

Some don't make enough money to make a fool of themselves.

Money can't buy love. It helps you shop for it.

Kids used to hide behind mamma's skirt- so did mamma.

A radical is usually right for the wrong reason.

Pretending to be rich keeps her poor.

The romance that ends over a leaky sink started over a water fall.

Golf liars have advantage over fishing liars. You don't expect the former to show any proof.

Why not wait until April to make a fool of yourself?

Liquor would kill germs, but they won't drink.

Why want God's blessings if you don't want God?

Linament helps when it hurts. So does the truth.

The trouble with people is people.

If the sentences were longer, the story of crime would be shorter.

You kick about the quality if you get something for nothing.

Stones are thrown at trees with fruit.

I don't trust one man because I don't know him; another because I do.

What sits up with a wife when her husband is late? Imagination.

Contentment thinks of yesterday without regret and tomorrow without fear.

Some women know the price of everything-the value of nothing.

Doctors will still make house calls if you have a telephone and Blue Cross.

Your life has no spare–Drive with care.

A man with manners and hair tips his hat to a lady.

The Lord (and IRS) must love poor people–He made so many of them.

You are what your husband has left after taxes.

Smoking gives your hands something to do–They shake.

Used cars are not bad as far as they go.

Justice for all is not divided evenly.

Last year she was voted the prettiest–this year the most popular–next year she will be voted the most stuck-up.

A well informed man's views are like mine.

When grandma's remedies disappeared, hospitals sprung up everywhere.

A self-made man should deny it.

A preacher scratches where members won't itch.

Some men want nothing and get what they want.

Why does a lawyer object as a witness tells the truth?

The man who believes he is a wit is half right.

A good stain remover is the blood of Jesus.

Save all your troubles until 3:00 o'clock. Then take a nap.

Our days are numbered with zip codes, area codes, social security figures and etc....

An embezzler is known by the company he clips.

A bus driver has his troubles behind him.

I never put off until tomorrow, what I can get someone else to do today.

The art of living is getting along with the people I don't like.

Glasses change your vision–if you drink liquor from them.

Only teenagers are too old to learn.

The shortest distance is under construction.

You are honest until you meet a temptation large enough to change you.

Good behaviour gets credit that should go to the lack of opportunity.

What flies fastest? Eagles on dollars.

It is easier to let the cat out of the bag than it is to put it back.

Marriage license is the biggest promissory note you will ever sign.

A woman sued for divorce-She said he he told her that he was a brick mason–He was only a bank president.

The lunar soil proves nothing can be raised on the moon but taxes.

Sometimes family trees have a shady branch.

If you pull a boner, you may have skeletons in the closet.

The wife's work that is never done is getting her man to assist her.

If ignorance was bliss, more folk would be happy.

The drawback to budding love is the blooming expense.

Some are not satisfied with what they deserve.

Many folk practice up for heaven if it is a place of rest.

Don't make an excuse you wouldn't accept.

A tender-hearted man hires an "efficiency expert" to fire people.

When it comes to school, kids object to the principal of the idea.

Why suffer in silence if you attract no attention?

We have one privilege left-Of doing without.

Some men are wise-Some are otherwise.

Give in the offering according to your tax report.

Most fur coats come from the male species.

There is a difference between nervousness and psycho-neurosis-Fifty dollars difference.

You are no bigger than the thing that makes you mad.

Today is the seed of tomorrow and the fruit of yesterday.

God formed Adam and sin deformed him.

A woman will overlook the rest of a man's life if he tells her that she is beautiful.

The world's disappointed man is the man that gets what's coming to him.

Make your own impression. Don't be a carbon copy.

Worry is to pull tomorrow's clouds over today's sunshine.

The bottom pan in a double boiler is always in hot water but never knows what's cooking. That is the way with some men.

What we do for God is not usually convenient.

In the matter of giving, some have short arms and deep pockets.

The easiest road always heads downward.

I'm one of the family-if God has died why was I not notified?

Why buy ice cream and reducing pills both?

The only limit to the power of God lies within the individual.

If you don't like policemen, the next time you are in trouble, call a hippie.

Some members are like straight pins – they point one way and head the other.

Religion is a good armor and a bad cloak.

White wash won't strengthen a fence- or a church member.

I am not what I think I am, but what I think-I am.

Jonah had himself a whale of a time.

Smoking may not send you to hell, but it may make you feel like you have been there.

Some don't appreciate the water 'til the well is dry.

The smallest deed is better than the greatest intention.

Hypocrites may keep you from going to church, but they can't keep you from going to hell.

WIFE: "Do you have an alarm clock that will awake the husband only"?

The temperature drops when you try to borrow cold cash.

God made light. The light company charges us for it.

A smile is a light in the window that let's us know you are home.

All kids could learn to write soon if they could work on fresh concrete.

You get out of a mirror what you put in it.

A popular sport is running...into debt.

If you are more stupid than 50 per cent of the people and less stupid than 50 per cent, you are average.

If things go wrong talk about how to fix it, not who is to blame.

To save money, some men forget who they owe.

We would deny it if we saw ourselves as others see us.

When we are old enough to know better we think we are too smart to get caught.

Blessed are the young for they shall inherit the national debt.

What teenage boys save on haircuts, they spend on hair spray.

Some secretaries are content after they find there is chance for advancement, raises, or marriage.

Some have ability to live beyond their income.

Around a Christmas tree is a family wrapped in one another.

We can't afford another depression with these prices.

A stupid idea can be dressed in pretty words.

I'm too old to repeat many mistakes.

People spend too much time crossing bridges that don't exist.

That which makes us become smaller as we grow great is called humility.

A man who is around when he needs me is a fair weather friend.

How can your faith be strong enough to get to Heaven if it is not strong enough to get you to church?

One man spent half of his time wishing for something that he could have been if he would have not used half of his time wishing.

Some pilgrims on the Lord's highway are only tourists.

Don't try to be better than other people. Try to be better than you were yesterday.

If you want to take weight off your mind, discard your halo.

A minister is like a candle, he consumes himself while he gives light to others.

Getting old is mind over matter. It does not matter if you do not mind.

If God stays awake, I'll go on to sleep.

What you do today affects the rest of your life.

You are a Sinner or a Saint - You are an "is" or you are an "aint".

It is not what a Christian belongs to, it is who he belongs to.

Sometimes nothing may be the best thing to say.

If your husband is so stupid, why did he marry you?

If your boss is so dumb, how come he hired you?

Bigamy is the only crime on the books where two rights make a wrong.

A man said that his wife is a human dynamo because she charges everything.

Many women can take a joke. They have one for a husband.

We never had it so good or parted with it so fast.

It is hard to break a habit or to keep from telling how to do it.

Why put a man in his place? Put yourself in his place.

When a man sings his own praise, he pitches his song too high.

Look comfortable if you want your wife's attention.

People are so tense these days, it's even hard to put them to sleep with preaching.

A blowout does not make you backslide - it's the slow leak.

Aren't you glad for your sake that no two people are alike?

Why worry? Half the lies people are telling on you probably aren't the truth anyway.

Repent of your past sins and those you intend to do.

Men die with boots on-the gas.

What is bad about age you get advice from your kids.

You decide to go in business- We decide if you remain there.

There is more business combined with pleasure than with profit.

Some fail trying to do good. Some succeed by accident.

If you don't like your job, another will.

There are things worse than being an old maid. Ask a wife.

In China, people have what the nation gives. We have what it does not take away.

Girls expose their legs. Boys expose their ignorance.

How does the wife like to be treated? Often.

A girl was looking for a man with a strong will-made out to her.

A man talked politics while he robbed a train-others do the same as they rob the taxpayers.

If you think you won't be missed, leave town owing a bill.

If you keep silent, no one can misquote you.

Five per cent of Americans do our thinking for us.

In America, we have the right to argue issues we don't understand.

A good executive can delegate responsibility and shift all the blame.

Sometimes the still small voice is fear.

The worst thing manufactured is an excuse.

A good example is better than good advice.

Secret sins don't usually stay secret.

Small people break relations with those who don't agree.

You'd be happy if you lost everything and suddenly got it back.

Educated women make good wives-their vocabulary explains why dinner is not ready.

Watch a half truth lest you get the wrong half.

Nothing needs reforming more than the faults of others.

Men play golf to keep from sleeping in church.

About the time I think I' m indispensable, I'm not.

Money does not make you happy, but it helps your creditors.

Years ago the police warned me to slow down-now doctors do.

If your son asks for the garage key, see that he gets the lawn mower.

The self-made men should have had some help.

The sermons on hell years ago are about like the ones on current events today.

Don't out maneuver the other drivers, outlive them.

A woman can keep one secret - Her Age.

If you want a thriving business, rent engagement rings.

The wife takes care of the inner man-husband takes care of the outer woman.

Television announcer: "A word from our sponsor who makes this show impossible".

Whether sharp or blunt, the tongue is a deadly weapon.

Over a million people are deaf, others just won't listen.

Don't side step your duty to greet temptation.

The generation gap is between the ears.

Your song will not be a hit if you sing your own praises.

It takes a lot of clear weather to lay aside for a rainy day.

There is one way to handle a woman-no one has found it.

The best things in life are free-the next best thing will bankrupt you.

When I think I'm bright, some want to polish me.

Advertising can be expensive if your wife can read.

Sign on a car: "Don't kill your wife. Let us do the dirty work."– B.A. LAUNDRY.

Sign on shoe shop: "Let us heel you and save your sole."

A tactful man will not change his mind, but will change his subject.

Do not be so busy doing the work of the Lord until you forget the Lord of the work.

Seven days without prayer makes one weak.

The worst mistake that I ever made was when I thought I made a mistake and didn't.

Consider the high cost of low living.

We need spiritual fruit rather than religious nuts.

The price of success is less than the cost of failure.

My best antiques are my old friends.

You are ripe for trouble if you are green with envy.

Children are excellent home furnishings.

A clear conscience is the best sleeping pill.

Fault is easy to find.

Some sit in church looking like they were baptized in lemon juice.

The favorite cereal of many teenagers is wild oats.

Since the world was here first, it owes us nothing.

Most men under rate what they don't have.

The smallest handcuff is a wedding ring.

Television does not take people from church against their will.

The busiest day of your life is often tomorrow.

I can't see for the suds when you soft soap me.

Ask God to strengthen your back - instead of lighten your burden.

A joke is dirty if it is doubtful.

A gravy train has no empty seats.

I only have three faults-what I do and what I say and what I think.

You may as well strike out as to stop on third base.

Four important words for some women are, I, me, mine, money.

The lazier you are, the more you intend to to later.

Why ask God to honor a draft if you have made no deposit?

The loafer has no loaves.

If your children are going down the wrong track, maybe they were not switched soon enough.

The greatest fault is when you believe you have none.

All drivers should be wide awake, alert and cautious; especially the one just behind the driverin front of you.

Words can travel faster than light.

Some people don't want to get their healing until they collect their insurance.

If you abuse your right to drive, it could cost you your right to live.

The IRS discriminates against people with incomes.

If you want to improve a man's hearing, praise him.

The trouble with the juvenile delinquent is apparent-Sometimes two parents.

You can't borrow yourself out of debt and neither can America.

United we stand - Divided we pay for a divorce.

It is better for drivers to be late here than early there.

You may cause men to forget the past with a present.

What can you give a man who has everything? A wife who knows how to spend it.

If you are sold on yourself, you still have to find a buyer.

Ants may have a circus, but termites can bring down the house.

Only teenagers are too old to learn.

Some workers don't think; some thinkers don't work.

There is one state that allows a woman to work eight hours-The state of matrimony.

We can't buy experience at a discount house.

When you get a little wind of something and turn it into a hurricane, that is gossip.

It takes a lot of pumping to keep some members inflated.

A hard way to take it easy is to fish.

I have a right to say what I please, but I have more sense.

If you had brains enough to run the college, you would not be a student.

We don't need a change in the work week, but in the weak work.

What causes matrimonial trouble is marriage.

Some are as lazy as they can afford.

When I repeat a joke, it reminds a preacher of a worse one.

Love is a self government under a two-party system.

No one wants to listen to your trouble except attorneys.

You don't know what you want but know you don't have it.

Men save the national debt for old age.

The covers are the best part of some books.

Mountains of worry built by mole hills of debt.

You don't object to trouble when it is disguised as money.

Read the instructions after everything else fails.

If you wear the seat of your pants out first, you must be an executive.

A curve you pitch that results in a hit-is a smile.

Candidates promise to move mountains, but only throw dirt.

A senator's definition of waste is money spent in another senator's state.

A device can now measure a millionth of an inch. It may be used for tax cuts.

Your weakest point is when a woman tells you that you are strong.

When you can't blame things on Uncle Sam, get married.

Some kids are slow learners-They are forty before they are a juvenile delinquent.

Two people realize their mistake, one keeps it and has to pay for it - That is called alimony.

We appreciate warm weather because the shirt is taxed off our back.

We spend more on kid's Christmas than on our honeymoon.

A man never appreciated real happiness until he got married, by then it was too late.

We buy cars that don't vibrate and chairs that do.

Laundry men take your suit to the cleaners. Lawyers lose your suit and take you to the cleaners.

Fishermen usually catch more after they get home.

Morticians have a lay-a-way plan.

An introduction is like perfume- not to be swallowed - it will evaporate in a few minutes.

Many times brains are on a furlow while the mouth is on duty.

Meals were thought out years ago-Now they are thawed out.

Some look for an occupation that does not keep them occupied.

You can economize easier when you are broke.

A form asked, "Length of residence at present address"? A woman filled out, "Ninety feet".

If we can't win the war against crime, we should have cease fire.

When you are bent on marrying, some lady will straighten you out.

A Christian who is satisfied with himself should pray through.

The woman who at one time had dishwasher hands, now have push-button fingers.

Teenagers know the answer to the problems they don't understand.

He waited for his ship to come in, but it was a hardship.

Those who really need advice seldom ask for it.

If you drive in 5: o'clock traffic, be careful you are not in the 6:00 o'clock news.

We don't whitewash ourselves by blackening others.

If you can look in a mirror and laugh, there is still hope.

Child care must first be learned from the bottom.

Why obstruct the billboards with highways.

Improve the world, begin with yourself.

Procrastination is the thief of time; so are all other long words.

A woman who makes sickness a pleasure is called a "nurse".

You never know what some men will say next–and don't know afterwards.

When my cup of happiness is full, some pain-in-the-neck nudges it with his elbow.

You hardly recognize your clothes when you take them out of the laundry–Or your girl when she comes out of college.

Profanity is strong words by weak people.

Having grandparents makes a kid smart.

The man who makes bank loans is not the same guy that writes the advertisements.

A person who can tell you all the details without knowing the facts is a commentator.

The man who won't forgive is the man in the wrong.

A good reputation makes some wonder what you are hiding.

If money talks–the dollar does not have enough sense to say much.

Time killing is a dreadful murder you can't recall.

Time is your friend until you try to kill it.

About all a business man can do on a shoe string is to trip and fall.

Take things as they come–If you can work that fast.

Nature has provided a way for you to interrupt your wife-You can sneeze.

Used to be the Fifty per cent of the married people were women.

Before you say too much about your teenagers, think who raised them.

How did you learn all the things you warn your kids not to do?

Failure makes news–Success makes history.

A self-made man denies the blame and claims the credit.

Memory reminds me I've forgotten something.

They have found a way to cut air pollution- a horse.

The future worries those who live in the past.

You get more for your dollar than ever before-more bills.

Asking too little of God will cause you to have to ask too often.

A man who is the head of the house is a bachelor.

Coffee used to keep people awake, now it is the price of it.

The "silent majority" is welcome to our church.

At one time a trip to the moon taxed only the imagination.

Some lead the way in a stony path. Others lag behind on the easy road.

It is not hard to get to the top if you can press through the crown at the bottom.

Some men are afraid of the unknown-They would be more afraid if it were known.

It's hard for a girl to find a boy attractive enough to please her and dumb enough to like her.

The church has many closed friends.

Optimists shake hands-Pessimists shake head.

Some long sermons don't reach far.

The wheel was a great thing until man got behind it.

We don't know the answer if we don't know the queston.

Some eat upside down cake and have an inside outhouse.

You will hear kind echoes if you speak kind words.

Some try to keep up their reputation and live it down.

You can't lose the victory-if you lost it, then it is not the victory.

Laziness keeps us from getting tired.

You can rise if you don't let tears blind you.

A woman's work is never done if she depends on her daughter.

Whiskey has many lovers and few friends.

Sometimes the know of the preacher ties a noose.

Why waste sympathy on yourself?

Your character is what you are in a crisis.

The hippies stopped people from bragging about their kids.

I appreciate my enemy. He tells me the truth when my friends won't.

A thrown rock can't be recalled - just like words.

If you tell a man he is all wet, you may get into hot water.

If you want to know how a cow feels after she is milked, pay your taxes.

Some people who break a habit save the pieces.

Most people can't afford to rest when they are young and don't enjoy it when they are old.

I could love humanity if it was not for the people.

The higher the mountain you climb, the better the view.

When a liar says nice things about me, he is easy to believe.

Many doubt their strength. Few doubt their importance.

If you want your name in the paper, read one while you drive.

Some look where they are going. Others see where they have been.

If I am really acquainted with myself, I don't wonder why I don't have more friends.

"Be yourself" is bad advice to give some women.

I'd rather aim and miss sometimes than to never shoot.

Alibi is the worst thing to buy.

It is better to let your imagination run away with you than to elope.

A middle-aged woman won't tell her age–and a man won't act his.

If all men did good, we would have no news.

Not all men who feel their oats use horse sense.

If you want to get down to the nitty-gritty, eat lunch on the beach.

Children disgrace us in public by acting like we do at home.

Computers can do more work-They don't stop to use the telephone.

If you don't worry about the world situation, you need your television examined.

College campus supports wild life.

Men grow tired hunting for rest.

Your life is bound together by business connections, family ties and golf links.

The next time you lost your temper or sight, don't hunt for it.

Courtship may be a question mark, an explanation mark, or a period before a sentence.

Years ago the men who wore blue jeans worked.

If you want to make a long story short, tell it to the elevator operator.

Switches keep trains from getting on the wrong track-The same is true for kids.

If you watch your step, you will get experience–also if you don't.

If you want to prevent sorrow, think today and talk tomorrow.

In America, there is the high cost of loving.

Some hear the whisper of temptation as it is heard above the loudest call of duty.

You don't make your dreams come true by over sleeping.

Parents never teach unless they practice what they preach.

You don't have to lie awake at night to succeed - Just stay awake days.

A good book that tells you where to go on vacation is your checkbook.

Plowing without sowing is like knowing without doing.

There is no use to sit up and take notice if you keep sitting.

Telling me a good joke reminds me of a dull one.

We don't notice what is cooking until it boils over.

"Truth or consequences" is an anti-cigarette commercial.

Blondes try to get ahead by starting at the top.

Sometimes the "silent majority" gossip the most.

A man who has two cars, a wife, and a son, is usually a pedestrian.

We can't lose weight by talking about it-keep your mouth shut.

How can a woman be president when she never reaches the required age?

When we get to be an old hand at the game, we lose our grip.

Cars keep owners strapped down without seat belts.

For Christmas some people get a new ulcer.

A back seat driver never runs out of gas.

Be careful, someone may take your advice!

You can guess a lady's age better without her help.

When there is a piano to be moved, I'll carry the stool.

You won't reach the right destination and go the wrong direction.

Columbus borrowed the money to establish that custom here.

If the grass is greener on the other side of the fence, the water bill may be higher.

A careful driver is the man who is behind the cop's car.

"Success" is two cars in the garage, a boat in the driveway, a note due at the bank.

Give yourself a blood transfusion. Take blood from one leg and put it in another-spill a little each time-you have an example of federal aid.

We like to see a good loser-if he is on the other team.

Many confused men think they are busy.

When all kids are in bed, a woman feels the joy of motherhood.

Old age looks back-youth looks ahead-the middle-aged look tired.

Distant relatives are best sometimes.

A man thinks as much of himself as you do of yourself as an "egotist".

We have courage 'till we need it.

Experience is "compulsory education".

Mini-skirts are okay if they are not on someone's wife or daughter or sister.

Wearing tight shoes help you forget your other troubles.

Sometimes poverty is partner to laziness.

In 1895, federal taxes were $1.98 per person. Now you pay more than that to a man who figures them.

I found that someon already knew the secret I was keeping.

A girl does her homework at the same time mamma does the dishes.

Someone will never get acquainted with God 'til you introduce them.

You can squeeze twice as many compact cars into a traffic jam.

Some people are taller in the morning and higher at night.

Talk is cheap if it is not long distance.

Why leave the clock minutes before your ship comes in?

The children try to bring up their parents in the way they should go.

Some people laugh to forget -others forget to laugh.

It would be good if success made the heart swell like it does the head.

Fast drivers beat the other fellow to the hospital.

If you could have your wishes, you'd double your trouble.

You know between right and wrong, but you hate to make decisions.

Somebody wants to be somebody - somebody wants to do somebody.

Parents of this generation talk like they had nothing to do with it.

A religion that does nothing is worth nothing.

One girl blushes when she is embarrassed - another is embarrassed when she blushes.

The four dimensions are length, breadth, depth, cost.

A good way to feel at home is not to leave.

If we are the light of the world, someone should use the switch.

If you can buy friends with money, they are not worth it.

Why does Uncle Sam wear a tall hat? He collects taxes on it.

Whisper words in church to get married-whisper in your sleep and get divorced.

In America, we can say that we want without thinking.

A fish grows fast after he is caught.

Don't order from a menu what you can't pronounce.

Some people can't hear an alarm as well as Sunday.

You don't need to know all the answers- You are not asked all the questions.

Half the men are under 30, all the women.

Some don't know what they are worth-some don't know what they owe.

Debtors have worse memory than creditors.

It is harder to live one sermon than to preach ten.

Prejudice looks for things which are not so hard that it can't see things which are.

We have peace on a war basis.

Give advice if you want men to notice your faults.

We are never as bad as some think; we are never as good as others think; we are always becoming what we think.

You will need a larger house if your kids marry.

The weather hinders the climate in our city.

If you don't get what you deserve, congratulate yourself.

The national anthem of hell is, "Everybody's doing it".

Why spend half your time wishing for things you could have if you did not spend half your time wishing.

DIET: If what you're eating tastes good...spit it out!

Even if you are on the right track, you may be run over if you sit down.

If a little bird tells you something, make sure it is not a cuckoo.

Be sure you have plenty of juice in your battery before you try to toot your own horn.

If you chisel in traffic, you may carve your own tombstone.

Gossip has no body or legs-it has many tales with a sting.

Cemeteries thrive if you drink and drive.

If a man who never heard of Christmas would watch you celebrate, what would it mean to him?

I owe my success to my difficulties.

Birds have bills and yet they sing.

A dollar looks small everywhere except in church.

If you have long standing troubles, try kneeling.

A rich man buys a nice home, then he buys a Cadillac to get away from it.

Flirting with sin can lead to romance.

The goods displayed in your window should be just like those on the counter.

It is what you learn after you know everything that counts.

If you think that you are going to wait until you can do something so well that nobody can find fault with it, *it'll never be done.*

One man went to church. He never missed a Sunday. The same man went to hell for what he did on Monday.

Death is not a period that ends the sentence of life. It is a comma to show there is more coming.

An anxious man prayed, "Lord, I want patience, and it want it right now!"

A man testified, "I was conceited. The Lord set me free. Now, I and the finest man you ever saw."

Beauty is skin deep - ugly is skin deep too.

Pick the right friends or the wrong ones will pick you.

Little people stumble over little things.

You cannot help men permanently by doing for them what they could and should be doing for themselves.

Choose your companions with care; you become what they are.

Treasure your time; don't spend it, invest it.

See what you can do for others; not what they can do for you.

Guard your thoughts; you are what you think.

Money can buy happiness if you want to spend it on others.

If other planets have people, foreign aid may go high.

Old salesmen never die. They just run out of commission.

Painting the pump won't purify the water.

Why spend money you don't have for things you don't need?

Pushing my luck slows me down.

On Christmas, I stay in to see how I come out.

When a man gets angry at his wife, he goes to the club-She reaches for it.

Worry crucifies you between two thieves-Regret of the past and fear of tomorrow.

When your ship comes in, there may be a dock strike.

Self-made men make their head too big.

Secrets aren't hard to keep, it's those blabbermouths that we tell, that spills the beans.

Instant replay is when she finds I have not listened.

There is no reward for finding fault.

If you have to practice what you preach, you'll prepare your sermons longer.

One secret is hard to keep-your opinion to yourself.

Vacations make time fly by-So do loans.

More kids would take after their dad if they knew where he went.

The doorbell has saved many family arguments.

Americans reach their goal with the help of loan companies.

Blessed are the kids that are too old to cry and too young to borrow the car.

If you want a raft of friends to keep you afloat, you are a free-loader.

To keep up a conversation, tell a little less than they want to hear.

All girl to her friend: All I am I owe to my dear Mother.
Friend: Then why don't you give her that 15 cents and get the debt paid?

The best of friends will wear out with constant use.

He that makes no mistake makes nothing.

Give a cat all it wants and it will not catch mice.

One woman does not have ulcers, but everyone around her does.

If you can't open it, tell a kid not to touch it.

You don't know what your life is worth 'til you pay alimony.

Run into debt and crawl out.

Love makes the world go-Money pays the bill.

Many times we get in a rat race and the rats win.

If you want to know if you have a good memory, try to forget.

The first few meals after marriage won't be perfect. It takes a little time to find the right restaurant.

We have plenty of money, but everyone owes it to others.

What did man descend from? What is he descending to?

If you want to go for a spin, take your wife and her charge card.

The only one worse than a quitter is the man who didn't begin.

If your temper gets you in trouble don't let your pride keep you there.

The one that gives you the most trouble is the one that wears your shoes.

A Baptist man refused to have a heart transplant because the heart came out of a Methodist.

Your ship will come in if you swim to meet it.

Man was made a little lower than the angels, but he fell a long way since.

If you want to know how many friends you have, buy a cottage on the beach.

Sign near a cafe; T-Bones 50 cents - Meat extra.

It is tough to pay so much for steak-The less we pay the tougher it is.

If time heals, then people should be healed waiting so long in the doctor's office.

The most expensive advice is free.

An air cushion is empty but it eases the jolt-It is the same with compliments.

You don't break the law, the law breaks you.

Some men are so afraid of getting out on a limb, they never climb the tree.

Gossip is ear pollution.

Ignorance gone to seed is called "prejudice".

Time passes quickly-Be ready when it passes.

A buzzard never comes around unless something is dead. Some people never come to church until someone dies.

We must be big enough to like people who do more than we do.

If you want to go to heaven study the road map.

I would rather say a good thing about a bad man than to say a bad thing about a good man.

You can't change the past but you can ruin the present worrying over it.

Character is what you are in the dark.

It is a short road to your wits end.

If you see good in people, people will see good in you.

We never find the day that is lost.

There are so many substitutes we forget what we first needed.

What used to cost $50.00 now costs $10.00 to fix.

The thing that one generation buys and the next generation discards, and the next generation buys again is an antique.

Sometimes women can hear better than men, but can overhear even better.

I like the woman that says what she thinks when she agrees with me.

The meek will inherit the earth–they support it now.

Weddings, funerals, and suppers help men attend church.

If you keep too much to yourself, you may be counted an embezzler.

If we profited by our mistakes, we would be millionaires.

Even a tombstone will say good things about a man when he is down.

While some folks are singing "Will there be any stars in my crown?" others are singing "No not one".

One group knows they have it, but are afraid that they will loose it–another knows they can't loose it, but they are afraid they don't have it.

One group really believes in divine healing, but they don't practice it; another group doesn't believe in backsliding at all, but they go ahead and practice it anyway.

While some are singing, "Plunge out into the deep" others are singing, "You are drifting too far from the shore."

Remember other people's goodness; forget yours.

Some men naturally have black eyes; others fight for them.

All we have seen of the dove of peace is her bill.

The woman that talks by the yard, and thinks by the inch should be removed by the foot.

If you blow your own horn you will come out at the little end.

Do not differ with the preacher's plans if you don't have better ones.

The audience that nods is not always agreeing with the minister.

Satan will run an "EXTRA" when a Christian goes wrong.

You have a right to do as you please if you please to do right.

Don't wait until you are dead to come to church.

Blunt words have sharp edges.

If you want to make the church better, start with yourself.

Why would a man have more dollars than sense?

Some folk really love the church if absence makes the heart grow fonder.

A diamond is a piece of coal that kept trying.

People who speak the loudest and longest say the least.

Money finds out how small you are.

It took a little while to get the Children out of Egypt, but forty years to get Egypt out of the Children of Israel.

If you have on the whole armour, you don't feel right in an easy chair.

One man said he had pride so he got in the prayer line, said"now thank God, I'm the best man in town".

Some people know more and more about less and less until they know a lot about nothing.

It is said, you use twice as many muscles in frowning than in smiling.

It is more fun to spoil your grandchildren than your own, since you do not have to live with them.

When most people want a pastor, they want one with the strength of an eagle, the grace of a swan, the gentleness of a dove, the friendliness of a sparrow, the eye of a hawk, the night hours of an owl; and to live on the food of a canary.

Paul withstood Peter to the face; most people can withstand preachers to their back.

If you would know the spirituality in living, check on your liberality in giving.

It is better to try and fail than to fail to try.

A little faith in a big God is better than a big faith in a little god.

The rush hour brings traffic to a standstill.

If you think your tax dollar does not go far, look toward the moon.

Some men fall for more than they stand for.

If at first you don't succeed, lay the blame on your wife.

Experience is the teacher that finds trouble with her pupils.

A banker goes on a diet because there is so much "collateral" in his blood.

If you don't know where you are going, you are lost.

If you loved your neighbor as yourself, he could not stand so much affection.

A footprint on the moon is not as necessary as a thumb print on the Bible.

Any girl can stop a man from making love to her if she marries him.

News men risk their lives to bring home a story-other men their lives with the stories they bring home.

If education helps us to earn more, why are school teachers underpaid?

The man who steps into a cage with a dozen tigers may be a bus driver.

Sixty years ago, we thought a man was crazy who went 25 miles per hour - it't the same today.

Some men acknowledge their mistakes - some defend them.

If you want to talk better in public, have something to say.

If you try to move from the table and the table moves - go on a diet.

Television has many lessons to teach, especially when you have one repaired.

Faith without corresponding actions is dead.

A bachelor has only his own dishes to wash.

A fool opens his mouth and empties his head.

Until your job means more than pay, it will not pay more.

Hippie: "If the shoe fits, steal it".

Breathe deeply if you don't care about your health.

Some towns are so little, they have mini outskirts.

He that moves mountains begins with small pieces.

Kids in school won't get interested in studying until sex education comes in.

Young men chase girls-Older men jog.

An optimistic husband went to the record building to see if his marriage license expired.

It is hard to find easy money.

At a party, some people spear olives and stab friends.

How does my wife expect me to think of her birthday when she never looks any older?

Two can live as cheaply as one if both have good jobs.

I remember when only rich folk paid income taxes and played golf.

We don't judge your faith by what you say about it, but what you do about it.

Nothing makes a child worse than belonging to a neighbor.

Children are a real comfort in your old age-and they make you reach it sooner.

The trouble with most children is that when they are not being a lump in the throat, they are being a pain in the neck.

Most children descended from a long line their mother once listened to.

Credit is a device that enables you to start at the bottom and go into the hole.

Advice for most young brides is on the top of the mayonnaise jar: "Keep cool, but do not freeze".

There is something unnerving about a kid with a Daniel Boone haircut, a Mark Twain mustache and an Abe Lincoln beard, telling us he is rejecting the past.

Charm is a way of getting the answer yes without having asked any clear question.

Some fellows give their wives a lot of credit cards, but the cautious ones give them cash.

A lot of people these days use sign language. They sign for this and sign for that.

Only the fear of God can set us free from the fear of man.

Some spend time counting the cost of following Christ, when they should consider the cost of not following Him.

A person can really become strict when he is dealing with other fellow's sins.

We die by living to ourself. We live by dying to ourselves.

It is better for a pot to boil over than to never boil.

The first few home-cooked meals are hard on a bride's nerves-and on a groom's stomach.

Newly weds discover that it takes a lot of juggling to balance the family budget.

There is trouble a brewing when matrimony becomes a matter of money.

Saying yes to a child is like blowing up a balloon-you have to know when to stop.

The greatest remedy for anger is delay.

Although children are deductible, they can be very taxing.

Heredity is what makes the mother and father wonder a little about each other.

Success comes to those who make the greatest profit from the fewest mistakes.

Whenever a modern child takes no for an answer, you can bet he asked a pretty shifty question.

Any child who is raised strictly by the book is probably a first edition.

You can tell a child is growing up when he stops asking where he came from and starts refusing to tell you where he is going.

Even children with the perfect table manners will spill the beans every now and then.

Contentment comes not so much from great wealth as from few wants.

Children are unpredictable-you never know what the neighbors will learn next.

The better the meal, the shorter the blessing.

The man who goes like sixty when he's twenty seldom reaches Forty.

The trouble with being an expert is that you can't turn to anyone else for information.

There is no hiding place in wider use, than in small print.

Wife to Husband: "Honey, will you still love me when I get old and grey?", "I reckon" said the husband, "I've loved you in all the other hair colors".

Does the going seem to be easier lately? Better check. You might be going downhill.

Architects designed picture windows to bring outdoors into a home. All you really need, however, is a couple of small children.

At sixteen, people think of only fortunes, at sixty, they think only of pensions.

Doctors tell us that hating people can cause ulcers, heart attacks, headaches, skin rashes and asthma. It doesn't make the people you hate feel too good either.

A man has just about had it when his weight lifting consists of standing up.

When Lincoln said, "You can't fool all the people all the time", the cloverleaf highway exit hadn't yet been invented.

Many a man goes into a bar for an eye-opener and comes out blind.

Intoxication is feeling sophisticated and not being able to pronounce it.

The hardest thing in the world to open is a closed mind.

In a bar, you start out fit as a fiddle and wind up as tight as a drum.

We must present a living Christ to a dying world.

The poorest man in the world is the man who has nothing but money.

Do you want to be cured of drunkeness? Watch a drunk man when you are sober.

Are you wise or otherwise?

Take D from the devil and you still have evil. Add O to God and you still have good.

If you don't share Christ, you cannot keep Him.

Two-thirds of promotion is motion.

Blessed are they that run around in circles, for they shall be known as "Big Wheels".

Think twice; then say nothing.

Life is a measure to be filled, not a cup to be drained.

If you want to break a habit, drop it.

If you can't change the past, but you can ruin the present if you worry over the future.

Worry is faith in the devil.

Remember, blank cartridges make a lot of noise.

The things that make us fret the most never happen.

Santa Claus finds himself in the red on Christmas, so do many of us.

Uncle Sam limits what we sow, except wild oats.

You will be ruined by the company you keep if you live for yourself.

The reason some folks get lost in thought is because it is unfamiliar territory to them.

If your children disturb the church service, give them what they want. If that won't do, give them what they need.

Even the teakettle sings, though it is up to its neck in hot water.

A man who says just what he thinks, should think.

Happiness adds and multiplies as we divide it to others.

Even a fish wouldn't get caught if it kept his mouth shut.

Every time a foreigner called a hospital to see how sick his wife was, they said she was improving. About the fifth day, he found that she was dead. He said, "What did she die of, improvements?"

Most churches need better deeds and less creeds.

We sing, "Sweet Hour of Prayer", then never show up for prayer meeting.

Some people sing, "There Shall Be Showers of Blessings", but they stay home from church if it looks like it is going to rain.

If you don't play to win, why keep score?

Some folk sing, "Have Thine Own Way, Lord", then pout if they can't have their own way.

No man is completely worthless; he can always serve as a horrible example.

Some people claim they want advice, but they really want some place to dump their worries.

Social tact is making people feel at home when you wish they were.

When you do not believe in yourself, that makes it unanimous.

Some preachers exhausts the subject. Some exhaust the audience.

Don't put off work 'til Labor Day.

How can you have an honest horse race without an honest human race?

If the going is easier, perhaps you are headed downhill.

The husband must allow for her shortcomings. She must also allow for his outgoings.

Why fight for more liberty until we use what we have?

Congress proves women don't do all the talking.

Many men look for work until they find a job.

If you have plenty to live on and nothing to live for, you are probably bored.

Truth becomes fiction after it is sold twice.

How many more years can Uncle Sam give away what he doesn't have?

Constructive criticism is when it's coming your way. Destructive criticism is when it comes my way.

When we get more machines to provide more people with more leisure so they can be more bored, that is called progress.

If you make more money than your son can spend, you are successful.

Filing cabinets is where papers gets lost.

We don't pay cash for knowledge. It comes in installments.

Hospitals are where men get bled.

It takes two years to learn to talk and forty years to keep our mouth shut.

Some has so many worries that a new one must wait.

It is thinking about the load that makes me tired.

If you believe half what a woman says, be sure it is the right half.

You don't know how many friends you have until you begin to prosper.

When a girl goes to the beach, she takes off as much as the law allows. It's the same in filing tax returns.

The less the government is worth the more it costs.

Kids are sure they will not be as stupid as dad.

Make stairs out of your stumbling blocks.

One man made a hearing aid for five cents. When he put a copper wire in his hear, people talked louder.

The man was counted out and did not hear the referee became successful.

The real thirsty kid has just gone to bed.

Some men get lost in thought. It's a new road.

It is stupid to worry about what you can help. It is useless to worry about what you can't help.

You don't observe the sabbath just by wearing your best clothes.

Money and secrets circulate rapidly.

When a man is successful, he gets the credit and his Uncle Sam gets the cash.

Every time I learn all the answers, they change all the questions.

A poor memory helps one to be happy.

An expert knows how to complicate simple things.

If you really know yourself, you don't wonder why you have so few friends.

Use your head more than your horn.

The girl that leaves home to "set the world on fire", returns home for the matches.

Parents used to kiss their kids good night. Now they can't wait up for them.

You can't keep a good-for-nothing man up, or keep a good-for-nothing man down.

A baby that can't lift its bottle can hold together a marriage.

None of the men who would make "perfect husbands" marry.

When the eraser wears out before the pencil, you've made too many mistakes.

God won't give a man a great reward if he gives away his overcoat in July.

Some women can't tell the truth without lying.

You will do too little if you are afraid you'll do too much.

Children leave one-by-one, but return two-by-two.

Medical science has improved. What was the itch is an allergy.

Ambition is rewarded with high taxes.

If you want to die poor, the IRS is ready to help.

How can we reform prison 'til we send better folk there?

Why don't they discover cigarette ashes to match the color of the rug.

If you want your child to be popular, give it a big hand-in the right place.

Having nothing to do tests your character.

The tighter money gets, the louder it talks. It's the same with people.

Women who dress to kill probably cook that way.

Silence can be guilt.

In the government machine, we have way too many nuts.

We have no quarrel with the institution of marriage, it is with the personnel.

Will power helps us not to read the other person's love letter.

Instead of poor preaching, maybe it was poor pay.

If it was a poor sermon, maybe you got your money's worth.

A church must not distribute religious aspirins.

Why pray while you keep one eye on temptation?

Your car has a longer guarantee than you do.

If half the people vote, it is usually not the right half.

Tomorrow is a labor saving device.

War does not show who is right, but who is left.

Economy planks in political platforms is wasted lumber.

The church is usually coin operated.

How can you keep His love warm with a cold shoulder?

If both parties get better mates than they deserve, the marriage is happy.

Politicians and kites are raised by wind and pull.

Husbands mourn over what they lose-Wives over what they never had.

To receive without deserving is worse than to deserve without receiving.

Spend your time getting ahead rather than getting even.

I can't blame circumstances for my character, or the mirror for the way I look.

Why try to keep up with the Joneses? Take it easy and you will meet them coming back.

Even a broken clock is right twice per day.

What we stand for, fall for, or lie for determines our character.

Unless people believe you, you can't be a successful liar.

If you can diagnose your case, you will know which specialist to see.

Most arguments have two sides and no ends.

Talk about me, you are a gossiper. Talk about yourself, you are a bore.

If you are ashamed of the past and afraid of the future, you won't enjoy the present.

To make money last, you must make it first.

If you use friendship as a drawing account, you should make a deposit sometimes.

If you can detour around rough spots, then take a trip down memory lane.

In D.C., pandemonium does not reign, it pours.

About the time I catch up with the Joneses, they re-finance.

We have freeways where several cars can collide at once!

A fat man has a place for his cigarette ashes to fall.

We know a man by what he does not say.

In one day marriage changes a good for nothing boy to a "Wonderful son-in-law."

One month Uncle Sam added 75,000 employees in an effort to reduce expense.

Sin springs a leak in the cup of joy.

Who would write our popular songs if we lock up all the feeble-minded hippies?

Lawns are so large these days, some men want two wives.

Taking the bull by the horn is not tooting your own.

Men have two worries-The end of the world and the end of the month.

It takes two years to learn to talk and forty years to learn to keep our mouth shut.

To put your point over without sticking people, is tact.

Some candidates shake enough hands to milk 100 cows.

The meek will inherit the earth before it is sold for taxes.

Sometimes an opportunity is camouflaged as a problem.

We say, "Don't worry". We should say, "Don't worry others".

When you gamble, you get nothing for something or something for nothing.

Johnny thinks he is allowed to pass everything if he passes his driver's test.

I read where a man made "Johnny" have some of his hair cut off, and found he was a neighbor's boy.

One man dreams of success–Another stays awake and succeeds.

What a girl knows is not as important as where she learned it.

Don't spend money foolishly for things you want, so Uncle Sam can spend it foolishy for things the other nations want.

To get a"new source of revenue", you tap the same taxpayer in a new place.

One man said, "I used to be conceited-God helped me over that. Now I am the finest man you ever saw."

One man said, "I promise never to exaggerate again. I know I have shed a barrel of tears over it."

You are successful when it costs you more to support Uncle Sam than to support your wife and kids.

It is more important to believe God than to understand Him.

An aim that seldom shows marksmanship is a budget.

I remember when students carried books instead of picket signs.

If you want to see a quick draw, open a joint checking account with your husband.

The only way some get through school is on a prayer. Now what will we do?

Little girl: "It pays to worry, for the things I worry about never come to pass."

You can't take your money to heaven, but you can send it on ahead of you.

Too many people are starched and ironed without first being washed.

You will not make yourself clean by soiling others.

Many people would not be in such a hurry to get there if they knew where they were going.

If you want to silence gossip, don't repeat it.

You can make people happy in some way; by coming or leaving.

Why carry a man to church, preach and sing over him after he dies, if he hates the church, singing and preaching while he is living?

Some people walk like they owned the town. Some people drive just like they owned the car they drive.

Some folks should sleep well; they lie easy.

The supply often exceeds the demand.

A great flame comes from just a small spark.

"Opened by mistake"- for letters or mouths.

Your sympathy is wasted if you used it on yourself.

We should not discuss evolution since the monkey can't defend himself.

A preacher does not need a bomb to kill a flee.

When your age starts telling on you, you stop telling your age.

If your brain is in neutral, your tongue will idle.

One way to quit tobacco is not to put it in your mouth.

In the day time we should be too busy to worry and at night time, too busy to sleep.

You should not brag on your former pastor if you helped starve him out.

It is easier for a girl to get married if she has a good job.

In marriage a girl gets a better half or poorer quarters.

Just because you fail in every line of work is no sign you are called to preach.

The first steps toward a successful life are the church steps.

The fellow who moves the world is the fellow the world can't move.

A loose tongue gets you into a tight place.

The kind of ancestors you have is not as important as the ones your children have.

Some people are so afraid they will make a mistake they don't do anything.

The people who speak of finding God in nature search for Him with a fishing hook.

There is no objection to what the pastor says if he says it in a few words.

If you want to know what is in a man's heart listen to his speech.

If some men had a good thought it would die from solitary confinement.

Some pastors are "pounded in", but kicked out.

Some preachers are too little for a big place and too big for a little place.

It does not take intelligence to find fault.

If you want to make ends meet, get off yours.

A wise man is not confused by what he can't understand.

Since the cancer scare, men borrow cigarettes.

If you have a poor memory and a poor imagination, you can be content.

If you don't know the value of money, try borrowing some.

Those who are of least value in the church are the hardest to please.

Truth is sometimes terrible. Look at the family album.

If I want trouble, I offer advice.

We don't like the shortcomings of our relatives or their long... comings.

Idleness does not travel fast. Poverty overtakes it.

Why stay at home because there are too many hypocrites. There is always room for one more.

How are trains and children alike? They both need to be switched sometimes to put them on the right tract.

Conscience helps. The fear of being caught helps too.

Who appreciated advice? The one who gives it.

Girls that show no common sense show most everything else.

Polite conversation is not to open your mouth until you have something to say.

Get up and open the door when opportunity knocks.

A critic would have you to sing it as he would-if he could.

The time to save money is when I have it.

You cannot keep out of trouble by spending more than you earn.

You cannot help men permanently by doing for them what they could and should do for themselves.

Choose your companions with care; you become what they are.

Treasure your time; don't spend it; invest it.

See what you can do for others; not what they can do for you.

It is better to be a poor man and a rich Christian, than a rich man and a poor Christian.

Better beg one's bread with Lazarus here, than beg water with the rich man hereafter.

Better to be the least in the kingdom of God than the greatest outside of it.

How can your faith be strong enough to get to heaven if it is not strong enough to get to church?

Some pilgrims on the Lord 's highway are only tourists.

Don't try to better than other people. Try to be better than you were yesterday.

One thing that you can give and still keep is your word.

If someone steps on your toes, you should not have them sticking out.

A minister is like a candle, he consumes himself while he gives life to others.

You can be a Pharisee or a Saducee or a "Glad-you-see".

Getting old is mind over matter. It does not matter if you do not mind.

Concerning the Bible, you should learn it before they burn it.

It is not enough to just be good- be good for something!

He who practices what he preaches will have to put in some over-time!

There are two kinds of people- those who lift and those who lean.

This fast age seems more concerned about speed than direction.

God shook the world with a Baby, not a bomb.

To grieve over sin is one thing; to repent is better.

It doesn't take any more time to say, "Good morning, Lord", than to say, "Good Lord! Morning."

Of all the things you wear, your expression is the most important.

In the matter of giving, some have short arms and deep pockets.

The easiest road always leads downward.

A man is also known by the company he avoids.

He who provides for his life, but takes no care for eternity, is wise for a moment, but a fool forever.

He who knows the way of the Lord can find it in the dark.

Some preachers are called, some chosen, some lukewarm, and others frozen.

I am not a man with great faith; I am a man with little faith in a great God.

The only limit to the power of God lies within the individual.

Men talk of brotherhood, but there are more hoods than brothers.

Some preachers are called, some sent, others just simply got up and went.

Jonah had a whale of a time - - literally.

One lady asked the preacher if she could get into Heaven with her Snuff, "I'm not sure", he replied, "But it's certain you'll have to go outside to spit".

Some come to crisis before they come to Christ.

A wife does not believe a pretty secretary can do as good work as others.

When you notice tact, it weakens.

I refuse to turn the grindstone for he who has an ax to grind.

An important trip is to meet your wife half way.

The narrow path and easy street do not intersect.

You don't feather your nest on a wild goose chase.

Recapture your youth - cut off his or her allowance.

We are in the same boat, even if we did not all come over on the same ship.

Quit giving yourself a pat on the back and give yourself a shove.

Liquor is not a way of life-but a way of death.

Some get up steam-others are filled with hot air.

Do you believe in the hereafter? The here determines the after.

If I buy what I don't need, I'll need what I can't buy.

The bouquet I hand to myself looks like weeds to others.

You don't realize a man is a fool until he loses his riches and honor.

The road to ruin is paved.

A man can differ with me without being crazy.

There are more insane people out of the institution than there are in.

The crowd need not know who spoke; they must know what was said.

Compromise is when two people get what neither of them want.

A wise tomato that knows her onions goes out with an old potato and comes back with a carat diamond.

You will not find the answer to your problem out side of God.

God gave us two ears and one tongue; so we should listen twice as much as we talk.

Some will sell you a car for a song if they can write the notes.

Do not trust a man too far, or a woman too near.

The bigger the man's head, the easier to fill his shoes.

The brook would lose its song if you took the rocks away.

Ninety-five per cent of what is done in the churches today could be done if there were no God.

Ninety-five per cent of what is done in the churches today is probably done by the faithful five per cent.

No one is as old as he hope to be.

Have you reached the age when you are losing a little on top? Well, cheer up! You are probably gaining in the middle.

Women seldom suffer from any given age-except when it is given by another woman.

The way we figure, the difficult age is when we are too tired to work and too poor to quit.

Folks never get too smart to learn new ways to be stupid.

There is no limit to what a man can accomplish if he doesn't care who gets the credit.

Some people want a preacher that is a good mixer. They need a preacher that is a good separater.

Some people want a preacher to deal with eternal things in just fifteen minutes.

Some people say, "I feel bad everytime I feel good, because I think about how bad I am going to feel when I quit feeling good."

You will know them by their fruits and not by their suits.

It is all right to possess money, but money must not possess you.

It does little good to shut the door after the horse is out.

The greatest load to carry is a pack of grudges.

Reckless drivers are not wreckless.

Be kind to your enemies because you probably made them.

I am not concerned about God's attitude towards you; I am concerned about your attitude towards God.

When a lost man makes the right correction, he goes the right direction.

A traveler may turn left and go right, or he may turn right and be left.

If we had more switches the children would need less clubs.

The man that knows it all has a lot to learn.

God does not altar the garments of salvation to fit you. Whittle yourself to fit the garment.

Jesus represents me in Heaven. I represent Jesus on earth.

You can be a good leader if you find some dumb people to follow.

A good wife and a surprised mother-in-law is behind most successful men.

A good preacher may not have his head full of facts, but he knows where to get them.

Keep the receipt when you pay for experience.

A pipe gives you high blood pressure-Trying to keep it lit.

Faith carries an umbrella when you pray for rain.

If you want attention, make a mistake.

Some did not spring far enough if they sprung from a monkey.

Some businessmen begin on a shoestring and end up at the end of the rope.

"The Yanks are coming", sings the dentist.

You make friends in prosperity–Lost them in adversity.

The only grounds for divorce is marriage in some states.

He that plays both ends against the middle is okay if he plays an accordion.

Some men look ahead-Some look disgusted.

A happy man helps his wife into her fur coat she bought while she was single.

I may not be paid for what I know, but I pay for what I don't know.

Your ship will come in while you sit-It will be a hardship.

Alcohol is not the problem. It is the men who sell it and drink it.

A politician who tells where he stands on public issues is tender-footed.

By the time you are proud, you think you are humble and you are not!

Patience helps me raise my eyebrows when I feel like flipping my lid.

An education helps one to get into expensive trouble.

If you have been shell-shocked, had a nervous breakdown, and shoot dope, maybe you can lead a rock and roll band.

If you have never failed, you've never tried.

Shoulder some responsibilities and you can keep your feet on the ground.

You don't run the risk of catching a cold in evening clothes-If you are a man.

Don't be broadminded about wrong things.

If you want to be successful, look happy when you are not.

Let the take-home pay stay at home.

A lady said someone stole $40.00 worth of groceries out of her glove compartment.

One good thing about ulcers, they cut our grocery bill.

Some men still have a voice-an invoice.

People are born faster than traffic can kill them.

In spite of inflation, wages of sin remain the same.

We improve everything but people.

Free advice is usually worth what it costs.

Modern music is so loud you can't tell which song it was stolen from.

It makes no difference if you can't tell the difference.

If sleep helps beauty, many women have insomnia.

The advice I give to others is hard to take.

If you just have to be ignorant, do it intelligently.

The school of experience has no free tuition.

Some wait 'til they find greener pastures, and then are too old to climb the fence.

Income tax would not be so bad if I knew to which country it is given.

Education helps you to worry over things others don't know about.

You are put in a tight spot by loose conduct.

The physician recommends pleasant thoughts while eating-with these food prices...impossible!

Some have car trouble. Car won't start. Payments won't stop.

Novels could be better if there was less cover on the book and more on the subject.

Most people are interested in what is none of their business.

Wisdom is knowing what to do with knowledge.

The world was made in six days without coffee breaks.

Farmers don't raise enough farmers.

In a small town, there is little to see and much to hear.

What is more permanent than a "temporary tax"?

Travel broadens the mind and lengthens the talk.

Later goes sooner after you pay now.

There is no hard work if you hire others to do it.

Those who make bikinis should be USA budget advisors.

A "middle of the road policy" causes car wrecks.

Progress is to go in circles, faster.

Money may talk, but a check tells IRS even more.

With all the insurance policies, why die a natural death?

The worst trouble with the human race is people.

Radio helps people with nothing to say-Talk to those who don't listen.

Some preachers boast of their dad because he raised such a great son.

Failures can tell me how to succeed.

The dollar today goes a long way, and gets there quicker.

People overseas are not stupid, they are just trying to imitate Americans.

Personal charm may win elections-It does not solve problems.

If your head goes straight, so will your feet.

If you want to stay awake during a sermon, preach it.

Just before the world blows itself up, you will hear an expert say, "It's impossible".

Some spend ten years in bars and fifty years behind them.

Many people still walk–to the carport.

This country stands for–Too much.

Young folk feel their oats-Old folk feel their corns.

Each year Americans grow taller-yet, they stay to their neck in debt and trouble.

American girls bait their hook for gold fish.

Maybe drug companies can make a "pill" to reduce spending by senators.

Fast cars bring two things closer together–This world and the next.

A secretary that does all the work should get half the credit.

It is said that bookkeepers don't get old, they just loose their balance.

Some look where they are going. Others just see where they have been.

Secretaries and wives mix like oil and water.

In a shoe store I called for some loafers–I was given one to wait on me.

The price on bacon has went hog wild.

It takes good eyesight to see your own fault.

A bride boiled an egg all day trying to get it soft.

The discussion has not necessarily ended when a man gets the last word.

Many people who work hard to try to make ends meed have an empty middle.

The Lord tries us with little to see what we would do with much.

No wonder some people are dog tired at night, they go around growling all day.

A little bird should be contented with a little nest.

Scientists prolong a man's life so he can pay all of his easy payments.

Luck is where preparation meets opportunity.

An armed robber makes you an offer you can't refuse.

Stand up and be seen. Speak up and be heard. Shut up and be respected.

Drive safely. Your car may not be the only thing that goes back to its Maker.

Money can't buy happiness, but helps you enjoy misery.

We are told, "If you are bald behind, you are a lover; if you are bald in front, you are a thinker; if you are bald in front and behind, you just think you are a lover."

The only way you can go while you are on the bottom-is up.

Is the fame of your preacher greater than the fame of our Saviour?

Some Christians read the menu but fail to order.

Don't give your report in battle until all the smoke clears away so you can see the results.

A preacher who depends on degrees will die by degrees.

A man noticed another in the store buying cigars, he figured a while then asked the man if he knew that if he quit smoking for a few years, he could own the hotel across the street. "Do you smoke, and do you own the hotel," the man asked, "No, I do" he replied.

Some people don't have much to say. You find it out after listening for an hour.

Do some repenting and do it quick, if your measurements won't come up God's yardstick.

Money once talked, then it would mutter–now it just leaves and doesn't even say goodbye.

It is nice to be important, but it is much more important to be nice.

If you have your head in the clouds keep your feet on the rock.

If we spend all our time getting even with people, we never get ahead.

Outward glory comes only from the inward light.

We pray mostly for ourself, but Jesus prayed mostly for others.

We can't expect God to remember the prayers we so easily forget.

If you don't profit from your mistakes, why make them?

You can't eat bread and loaf too.

It is better to keep your mouth shut and let people think you are ignorant, than to open it and show them you are.

One preacher was praised for not watching a clock, but yet being able to stop preaching at exactly 12:00 every Sunday. The next Sunday he preached until 3:00 p.m. The minister was called before the Board for an explaination. He replied, "I usually put a cough drop in my mouth at the beginning of my message and close my message at the time the cough drop is gone. I think I must have reached in my pocket and found a button instead".

A family next door to a widow with six children was curious and asked why she whipped each of her children every evening when she returned and she replied, "I don't know, but they probably do".

The exercise that some people take is jumping to conclusions.

He who toots his own horn runs down his own battery.

There has been no reduction in the wages of sin.

Killing time is not murder; it is suicide.

We must not be more concerned about speed than we are about direction.

In algebra, X is something that is unknown, that is why some people write Christmas as Xmas.

Those who think they can't are usually right.

If you want to make a dream come true; wake up.

Today is the tomorrow you worried about yesterday.

You can put your best foot forward without kicking.

Christian warfare doesn't always determine who is right, but who is left.

It isn't what you would do with a million if riches would ever fall your lot; it is what you are doing for Jesus with the dollar or the quarter you have got.

A smooth sea does not make a skillful sailor.

Regardless of what the Supreme Court says, there will be prayers in school as long as there are exams.

Some people suffer from a run down physical exhaustion. Others suffer from a "wound up" hypertension.

Religion is earthly. Salvation is heavenly.

Religion is what man does for God. Salvation is what God does for man.

The average American taxpayer thinks he has his nose to the grindstone when really he has his back to the wall.

With all these commercials on television, it makes a parent feel kind of silly punishing a child for lying.

When a wife starts wearing the pants in the family, the husband usually shops around for a new skirt.

Permitting a woman to have the last word doesn't require courage -but it sure takes a lot of patience.

Most of us wouldn't have such fat wallets if we would remove our credit cards.

In the Sweet Buy and Buy - is the credit card.

To increase the value of gold, have it handled by your dentist.

If you insist on looking down in the mouth, take up dentistry.

In the old days, marriage used to be a sacred contract. Today, it is more like a ninety-day option.

As soon as a girl gets her divorce, she gets back her maiden aim- to get a new louse of life.

A man's home can be his hassle.

Some folks consult a masseur or a chiropractor when they want to get rid of a pain in the neck. Others get a divorce.

Having a big family around is a good way to make sure there'll always be someone to answer the phone and forget the message.

A husband is a bachelor who solicited directions.

The honeymoon is over when the fellow who won his bride with soft soap winds up washing the dishes.

Any husband who is right better have an apology ready.

We should spend our energy giving reasons for that which ought to be done, instead of excuses for the things left undone.

The trial that makes us fume and fret, the burden that makes us groan and sweat, are usually things that haven't happened yet.

It takes longer to explain why we done things wrong, than to do them right in the first place.

The middle letter of Pride, Lucifer and Sin is "I".

Juvenile delinquency has increased since there have been so many woodsheds converted into garages.

Some people think a thirty minute sermon is too long, so they substitute hours of television programs for it.

A librarian said people may be poor mathematicians, but they are all good bookkeepers.

Todays mighty oak is yesterdays little acorn, that held its ground.

When God touched Jacob's thigh he had power with God: he got his pocketbook converted.

Wisdom is knowing what to do next; skill is knowing how to do it; virtue is doing it.

After all is said and done, it hath been the woman that said it, and the man that done it.

If you give you are the boss of money; if you don't give, money is your boss.

What was it that you were worrying about a year ago?

I have never heard anything about the resolutions of the apostles; it was about the acts of the apostles.

The only difference between stumbling blocks and stepping stones is the way that you use them.